No Birds Singing

Recent Titles by Vivien Armstrong from Severn House

BEYOND THE PALE
CLOSE CALL
DEAD IN THE WATER
FLY IN AMBER
FOOL'S GOLD
REWIND
SMILE NOW, DIE LATER
THE WRONG ROAD

No Birds Singing

Vivien Armstrong

Severn House

This first world edition published in Great Britain 2003 by
SEVERN HOUSE PUBLISHERS LTD of
9–15 High Street, Sutton, Surrey SM1 1DF.
This first world edition published in the USA 2003 by
SEVERN HOUSE PUBLISHERS INC of
595 Madison Avenue, New York, N.Y. 10022.

British Library Cataloguing in Publication Data

Armstrong, Vivien
No birds singing
1. Murder - Investigation - England - Oxfordshire - Fiction
2. Detective and mystery stories
I. Title
823.9'14 [F]

ISBN 0-7278-5984-6

Typeset by Palimpsest Book Production Ltd.,
Polmont, Stirlingshire, Scotland.
Printed and bound in Great Britain by
MPG Books Ltd., Bodmin, Cornwall.

One

It was Tansy Robotham who found the body.

Propping her bike against the front wall, she rang the bell. The house was in darkness, a glossy magazine poking through the letterbox, the garage door closed down. Tansy slipped through the side gate and, shining the headlight from her bike, opened the conservatory door, meaning to stash the beauty pack in the cupboard under the sink as usual.

It was already dark, the early autumn days drawing in, curtains pulled against drifting fog. A misty half moon gleamed through the elms which bordered the lower end of the village. Tansy wished she'd been able to pop in earlier as she had planned, but the darned washing machine repairman had let her down and she'd wasted the entire day hanging about the house, making fruitless calls to the mechanic. 'Lucky I brought the lamp from the bike,' she muttered to herself, a precaution against the thieving louts who had pinched the lights from her bike once before when she'd been calling on a customer. The conservatory was pitch black, even the feeble moonlight shut out by louvred blinds.

She shone the light across the tiled floor to illuminate the corner where she usually left the deliveries when Sandy was out. Her trainers skidded and, for a moment, she almost lost her balance. But it was only as she rounded the rattan sofa that the crumpled body appeared in the narrow beam. Sandy's face was turned towards her, whisps of white-blond hair matted against her cheek, clots of congealed blood blackening her temple, a manicured hand covering her throat. But it was the dead woman's empty eyes staring up as if in disbelief that struck like a blow to the heart.

She screamed, and stumbled into a low table knocking a wineglass on to the floor, where it shattered into fragments. Grasping at the empty air, Tansy dropped the lamp, and, slithering in the slime she knew to be blood, fell to her knees amongst the broken fragments, paralysed with fear.

But she was wrong. A path of light streamed across the floor, spotlighting the ultimate horror. The slime, only inches from her face, was revealed as the squashed remains of dozens of tiny maggots. Others moved across the dead woman's head, into her eyes, crawling between her fingers, soundlessly dropping on to the ceramic tiles.

Tansy's cries reverberated under the dark apex of the glass roof like the screams of a vixen caught in a trap.

Two

Chief Inspector Roger Hayes had customized his new office, one of the perks of promotion. His predecessor's accessories: the silver trophies, the badly focused photographs of the Lake District, the pungent smell of menthol cigarettes – all gone. The shadowy reminders in the way of unfaded squares of paintwork on the walls were all that remained of Billy Duveen, now retired with his fishing tackle and nice comfortable wife, well shot of the ups and downs of a patch centred twelve miles from Oxford and encompassing extensive farmland estates and commuter villages near enough to London to make the journey to the city a reasonable choice.

DCI Hayes had no wife and no fishing tackle. A divorcé, thirty-five years old, and one of those 'terriers' whom the old guard continued to regard as 'too clever by half', Hayes' eyes were set on the fast track to the top and his lack of a wife, especially the wife Patsy Hayes had turned out to be, could only be an advantage.

His sergeant, Bellamy, pushed through the open door, his normally careful approach to the new boss sharpened by anticipation of a break in the dull routine of traffic offences and punch-ups outside the pubs and clubs in Renham on a Friday night.

Hayes looked up, frowning. 'Yes?'

'Nine-nine-nine call, guv. Just come in. Some woman's been murdered in Newton Greys.' He smothered a burgeoning smirk. That'll wake the bugger up for sure.

'Newton Greys. Isn't that the village where there was all that palaver about the public footpaths?'

'Right, sir. Local squire, calls himself Major Vennor, got stroppy with the ramblers on his land. This woman they found dead was living on one of the new housing developments.'

'Well, what are we waiting for? Let's go. The SOCO team's been alerted?'

Bellamy drove the Chief Inspector to Sandy Prentice's house in less than fifteen minutes, their arrival adding yet more clangour to Didcot Drive, a cul-de-sac featuring only six houses, each, in Hayes' estimation, a blot on the landscape. They were, he was told, less than two years old and part of an estate built in design permutations of mock-rural charm popular with young families and retired folk with a decent income. The dead woman occupied number 6, nearest the exit, the other dwellings a mixture of bungalows and detached houses ranged around a central shrubbery.

Hayes shoved past the police cordon and spoke to the constable on the gate of number 6, a man all too familiar as the unlucky recipient of a bollocking from the new boss on his first day at the Renham station.

'Who found the body, constable?'

'A girl delivering make-up. A Mrs Robotham. She's with the neighbour at number five. He was out with his dog and heard the screams and –'

'The victim?'

'No, the woman who found the body. He took her back to his 'ouse and phoned nine-nine-nine. WDC Robbins is with them now.'

'Who's here?'

'The local bobby, a bloke called Frame who lives in the village. And the pathologist's just arrived. The police doctor's with him now.'

Constable Rudd looked wary, as well he might, Sergeant Bellamy decided, the men at the station already blowing hot and cold over their new DCI, a man with a short fuse and a curt manner. Mind you, it was early days, Bellamy admitted, and the real reason for Hayes' transfer from Oxford had yet to be established in the chit-chat in the canteen.

The house was all aglow, the place lit up like party night. The front door stood ajar and, careful to keep his hands to himself, Hayes hurried inside.

The narrow hall revealed several open doors, the main room leading through french windows into the conservatory. The doctor looked up, a middle-aged cynic with not much hair but a wealth of experience. For a medical man his abhorrence of gore was an increasing difficulty, violent bloodshed of pretty girls being acutely painful to him. Dr McKenna blamed his wife's addiction to TV cop shows for this awkward sensitivity, the rawness of even fictional lives now almost commonplace and regrettably no longer the stuff to give the viewers nightmares.

In real life the blood-letting was ugly, and the tragedy of the sprawled victims, even those he more commonly encountered in the investigation of road accidents and street fights, he viewed with distaste. Maybe he was getting too old for this job. Certainly, eager young inspectors like Hayes seemed to be energized by the drama of a killing like this.

He straightened, pulling off his gloves, eyeing Hayes with curiosity.

The inspector held out his hand. 'Good evening, doctor. We've not met. My name's Hayes – I'm new here.'

'Yes, I heard.' He turned away to pack his bag. 'I'll leave you in the capable hands of our pathologist here, Dr James. Luckily he was in the area so you're off to a brisk start,' McKenna said, nodding briefly at his medical colleague before stepping smartly into the back garden. Hayes and the man he reluctantly characterized as 'Doctor

Death' moved into the living room where James shed his protective clothing.

James was very tall, very thin and astonishingly smartly turned out for a man called out on an emergency call from his warm fireside. On second thoughts, the warm fireside sounded much too cosy for Hector James, Hayes concluded, a man whose narrow gaze presumably focused daily on the human debris of life.

'What's the story then, doctor? Time of death?'

Three

The pathologist laughed thinly, indicating the scattering maggots infesting the body.

'Well, these little fellows will probably help with that. Do we know if these conservatory doors were open when the poor woman who found her arrived? The temperature's important and as I'm no expert on maggots I've phoned a colleague of mine to have a look-see before the body's moved. You've no objection? He's already on his way.'

'From where?' Hayes gloomily calculated the fees an extra medico was likely to add to the cost of the investigation.

'Oxford.'

Hayes shrugged, eyeing the cadaver with renewed interest. Bellamy coughed, looking distinctly nauseous. 'On his way, you said. How long before he's likely to get here?'

'Half an hour at the most. He can't wait to view our poor lady here. His name's Professor Glyn. The orchids in here would need a constant temperature – at a guess I'd say death occurred at least ten days ago.'

'I'd better talk to the neighbour who took in the woman who discovered the body. May I leave you with this while you instruct the SOCO team? I'd like to get the story from her before there's any loose talk between them. Won't be long. Don't go before I come back, OK?'

Hayes hurried out without waiting for a reply, telling his sergeant to stay at the scene while he nipped next door.

He hesitated at the garden gate, swiftly taking in the layout of the oval cul-de-sac with its six houses, all glossily painted up like scrubbers out for a night's clubbing. The victim's house occupied a triangular plot and seemed larger than all but one of the others. He made for the bungalow next door, its neat front garden fenced with spindly privet, 'Mon Repos' painted in defiant script on the gate swinging back and forth in the chill wind. A dog started to bark inside, launching itself against the door as he rang the bell.

The WDC answered, holding back a feisty little terrier. It was a girl he remembered seeing at the station, Robbins, someone they called Gilly or Sally, something like that. She closed the door behind him and he caught her sleeve as she bent down and tucked the dog under one arm.

He lowered his voice. 'You been here long, Robbins?'

'We responded to the nine-nine-nine call. First on the scene.'

'What's the score? The woman, Mrs Robotham? The one who found the body. Not gossiping with the neighbours, I hope?'

'Oh no, sir! She's still pretty hysterical – I think she should see a doctor. She's been throwing up like a seasick sailor. We've hardly been able to get a word out of her, practically off her trolley with shock.'

'She hasn't talked about it? Not said anything about the bloody maggots?'

'No. Just keeps asking to go home. Her mum's babysitting, apparently.'

'Right. Thanks. Let's try and get some sort of brief statement, shall we? It might be useful to get her away from here before she starts blabbing. I don't want the press broadcasting the murky details too soon.'

Jenny Robbins nodded. 'She lives in one of the cottages by the post office, she said.'

An elderly man in a Fairisle cardigan hurriedly emerged

into the hall and snatched the dog from her arms, shutting it in the kitchen before inviting them through.

Hayes and Robbins stepped into the small sitting room, glancing round at the set-up. The old man closed the door behind them and introduced his wife, who sat on the sofa next to Hayes' chief witness, a thin girl with stringy hair and eyes drowned in despair and terror. He flashed his ID and smiled stiffly at the two women, the man of the house gazing at his unwelcome visitors with glum acceptance. A log fire blazed in the hearth, the heat of the room almost taking his breath away.

'Mrs Robotham?' he enquired. They were both tearful, the younger one wild eyed, the elderly party clearly upset. She patted the girl's hand, pressing a box of tissues towards her as the DCI advanced to sit in a straight backed chair he pulled away from the dining table. The policewoman hovered by the door, watching Hayes.

Hayes softened his voice and murmured sympathetic phrases, gradually lowering the charged atmosphere with his tone of genuine concern.

'You need to get back home, I know. Shall we just get a few facts straight and then I'll get my colleague here to drive you?' He motioned Robbins to move in closer and signalled her to take notes.

'Let's get some information on paper, shall we? Your name, young lady?' She blew her nose but, brightening, spoke up, her voice barely a whisper.

'Tansy Robotham.'

'And your address?'

'Three Low Road.'

'Now, in your own time, tell me what happened, Mrs Robotham.'

'Actually, it's Miss. Miss Robotham, see?'

'Oh, right . . . Not important but just as you wish, Miss Robotham. Now, what time did you arrive next door?'

'Getting on for six. Can't be sure but Mum was watching *Richard and Judy* on the telly when I left and I had a pile of calls to make. I asked her to pop round to look after my little boy while I made some deliveries, beauty stuff – I work from home. Star Cosmetics, you know it?'

Hayes smiled encouragement.

'Well, I called in at Mrs Foster's with her face masks and a hair spray, made a couple of trips to the council estate, then up to the pub to leave an order with Mollie, and after that I biked over here with Sandy's stuff. I mostly leave Sandy's till last and then we have a bit of a natter and a cuppa and sometimes she gives me a trim and a blow-dry for free.'

Her voice faltered, fresh tears brimming as she gripped the elderly woman's hand.

'I know this is painful, but just the bare facts will do for now. You can make a full statement in the morning, but if I may press you to continue, Miss Robotham?'

'Shall I make a pot of tea?' the old man interjected, his horror at the terrible turn of events clearly etched on his sagging cheeks.

'Not now!' Hayes barked, then, moderating his response, 'Later, thank you. But I must get on if you don't mind.' He nodded at the wretched girl on the sofa who struggled to relive the trauma.

'Well, er . . . OK. The place was all dark, see. I wasn't surprised. Sandy often went away for holidays and stuff. She worked all over the place an' all, London sometimes but mostly round Oxford.'

'She was a hairdresser?'

'Yeah, but not in a shop. She did ladies in old people's homes, hospitals sometimes, posh places, private, you know, expensive . . .' The words trailed off and tears started to fall.

Hayes looked pleadingly at Robbins who hurried out and returned with a glass of water.

After a few moments, Tansy recovered a little and went on.

'When Sandy's out I leave her order in the cupboard under the sink in the conservatory. The house is alarmed but she leaves the garden door unlocked and—'

'I keep an eye on the orchids,' the old man put in, 'and Sandy leaves a set of keys with me in case of emergencies. She was away a lot. I gave the keys to the police officer.'

'Ah yes, Mr er . . .'

'Mason, Frederick Mason. We all moved into Didcot Drive within weeks of each other so we're all very friendly. Help each other out, you could say.'

'I feed Mrs Harris's cat at number one when she's off visiting her son,' his wife swiftly added, nodding agreement with the old man, keen to make it clear to this interrogator that Didcot Drive was a respectable little enclave with nice friendly neighbours. 'Oh dear.'

The girl started sobbing, ugly retching sounds which set the dog off again, barking its bloody head off in the kitchen.

Hayes lifted an eyebrow at Robbins and rose. 'I think that will have to do for the present. I have to speak to the pathologist but perhaps we could continue this later, Mr Mason, just to verify the facts. I think Miss Robotham has had enough for one day.'

He turned to the constable. 'Run this young lady home, would you, Robbins? And then get back here sharpish – there's a lot to get through tonight. I'll get Bellamy to come in here with me later and we can hear Mr Mason's side of the story.'

The harassed looking trio rose as if on cue and Jenny Robbins took the girl's arm to lead her out but she shook her off, shouting:

'My bike! I can't leave my bike!'

Hayes made a swift exit, slamming the front door behind him.

Four

Hayes extracted his sergeant from a chin-wag with the constable on the gate of the Prentice house, and went inside.

'The expert from Oxford's only just arrived, guv. The pathologist said it could take some time.'

Hayes pushed open the door into the conservatory. Dr James and Professor Glyn were hunched over the body, conferring quietly, keeping the SOCO team at arm's length. They both looked up, frowning, and Hayes decided to take the hint and get straight back to the Masons.

'Right. Well, we'll leave them to it for now. Come on, Bellamy, I want to talk to our other witnesses on their own before the story gets mangled.'

They hurried back to the bungalow. The door was still on the latch, the dog still yapping. Mason beckoned them into the sitting room. They were alone, still shell-shocked by the terrible turn of events, the woman now more accepting, distracting herself with small tasks in an effort to ward off the horror of it all. She bustled about, setting out teacups and biscuits on the coffee table, the old man looking alarmingly green about the gills. Hayes introduced his sergeant and sat down, accepting a steaming cuppa with a nod. Bellamy opened his notebook, eager as a truffle hound.

Fred Mason subsided into his Parker-Knoll by the fire, the logs falling inwards with a shudder of sparks and dying embers as Hayes began his questioning.

'Now, shall we continue, sir? Just a brief résumé, we can get a full statement signed in the morning.'

The old man dabbed his mouth with a handkerchief and adjusted his spectacles, his voice now firmer, his manner more composed since the Robotham girl had been whisked away.

'It was just before six. I was in a bit of a rush to get back from my dog walk in time to catch the news. As I turned into the Drive I heard this terrible screaming next door. I thought it was Sandy – well, you would, wouldn't you?'

The wife looked increasingly anxious, watching poor Fred with pursed lips, hoping this terrible thing that had happened wouldn't bring on one of his nasty turns. High blood pressure was no joke at their age.

Hayes nodded hopefully, sipping his tea, attempting to seem relaxed and unhurried.

'Well,' Mason continued, 'me and Brandy – the dog, you know – ran round the back to see what was up. It was black as pitch and that poor young woman, Tansy, was howling like a banshee, crawling about in the dark trying to find her way out.'

'It wasn't possible to put on the lights in the conservatory?'

'The switch is inside the house. As I told you I keep a set of keys for Sandy in case of emergencies when she's away – frozen pipes or something, you know . . . But the house is pretty well burglar proof. Sandy has a lot of nice things, a stereo system and valuable knick-knacks, china figurines, the sort of thing women like.'

'So you didn't go inside the house and put on any lights?'

'Didn't have the keys on me, did I? Why would I expect any trouble next door? And when I check round when Sandy's away I do it in daylight, no need to go right through unless I think there's been a break-in or something.'

'So you found Miss Robotham screaming in the dark. And?'

'Could barely see your hand in front of your face and the dog was in a terrible state an' all, barking his head off and straining on his lead like a bloodhound.'

'You helped her up and tried to get her to talk?'

He shook his head, nervously smoothing his moustache. 'No chance of that. The poor girl was terrified, couldn't get a sensible word out of her. It struck me she'd been frightened by a rat in the dark, silly girl, so I grabbed hold of her and pulled her back to the bungalow, hoping Meg could calm her down.'

'You didn't see the body?'

'No, thank God. I think Brandy did though – I had the devil of a job dragging Tansy and the dog back here; the girl was practically fainting with fright. She only blurted out what had happened when we got back here.'

'And then you phoned for the police.'

He nodded. 'I hardly believed what she was saying, but you think Sandy's been murdered?'

'Oh yes, no doubt about that. Did Mrs Prentice have men-friends to the house, do you know? A regular boy-friend even?'

'Sandy had a lot of admirers,' the old lady put in, 'and why not? She was a handsome woman, and full of fun. Used to be away a lot though, through her job, and holidays, of course.'

'But she didn't confide in you about anyone special, Mrs Mason? A little romance on the side perhaps? A secret visitor? Someone in the village even?'

She shook her head. 'Very occasionally she cut men's hair at home – in that conservatory place, there's a proper sink and hand shower and everything. But only as a special favour.'

'Her work was elsewhere.'

'Nursing homes, and a few private customers, housebound ladies who like to look nice, you know, but can't get out and about very much.'

'It must have been a lucrative little business,' Hayes ventured.

'She had private money,' Mason put in. 'Family money, an inheritance, she said.'

'Was she widowed? Divorced?'

'Divorced.' The old lady was loosening up, recovering from the aftershock of a murder on the doorstep, the death of a friend from some unknown assailant who was probably still at loose in this quiet backwater. 'She once told me an aunt left her a house in London and her life savings. Lucky you, I thought at the time. But you couldn't begrudge Sandy a bit of luck. She was so full of life, Inspector, so cheery – a real tonic, to be honest.'

'And this busy person with a job and a full social life did her own housework?'

'Of course she didn't. Why should she spend her time dusting and cleaning?' she said, glowering at the old man slumped at the fireside. 'She had young Melanie from the village to do everything, even the laundry, and Jim Loxley did the garden.'

Hayes perked up. 'You know her, the cleaner?'

'Melanie Crabbe. Lives on the council estate off Church Lane. With her "partner" as she calls him, a right layabout called Jason, one of those scroungers in and out of the post office every week collecting his dole money.'

'And the cleaner hasn't been in?'

'Couldn't say. We've been on holiday for the past fortnight.'

'Does Melanie have keys when Mrs Prentice is away?'

'No, never,' Fred interjected. 'Sandy didn't trust her. Told me she made sure she was at home when Mel came round on Wednesdays.'

'She was thinking of giving her the push,' the old lady confided. 'Sandy said she'd sooner do the work herself, but I couldn't see it myself. Sandy wasn't the type, not your average housewife if you see what I mean.'

'So you didn't know Mrs Prentice hadn't been seen for over a week?'

Mason looked up, his eyes focusing defensively. 'No. Why should I?'

'But you looked after her plants, you said, when she was away.'

'She never told me she was going away. Anyway, Meg and I couldn't have helped out, we only got back from our holiday yesterday. Picked up the dog from the kennels this morning, did a bit of shopping and then this happens!' He sounded petulant, as if Fate had played a dirty trick, spoiling what had been a nice autumn break. 'We were on a cruise,' he added: 'Norwegian fjords.'

'And very nice too. And the other neighbours gave no indication Mrs Prentice had apparently been away?'

'Not a word. She loved those plants, you know, wouldn't go off without making sure I could keep an eye on them.'

'Valuable?'

'Not really. But lovely things to have. Sandy had green fingers, you know. Grew all sorts of exotics in that conservatory. Had heating put in specially, a misting system, the lot. Almost no trouble at all really but a pricy hobby. Not that she was short of a bob or two.'

'But she always asked you to keep an eye on things for her when she was away from home?'

'That's what neighbours are for, Inspector. No man's an island, as they say.'

'She paid you for all this neighbourliness?'

Fred drew back, clearly affronted. 'Of course not. It was the least we could do. She was generous in her way, gave a lovely drinks party last Christmas for all the people in

Didcot Drive, kids and all, not bothered about standing on ceremony.'

'You liked Mrs Prentice – Sandy?'

'Very pleasant young lady.'

'Not really so young.'

Fred laughed. 'Young as far as we're concerned, Meg and me.'

'No trouble in the village? Jealousy? Comment about a sexy-looking single woman moving in?'

He shook his head, nonplussed. 'Sandy got on with everyone – even the people at the big house, Major Vennor and Lady Honora. And she played the piano for the vicar's charity concert in the village hall in July. No, Inspector, Sandy Prentice was starting to be a real asset to Newton Greys and "incomers" as the locals call us, are not always welcome, believe me.'

The doorbell pealed. Hayes motioned Bellamy to go see and a murmured conversation filtered through to the sitting room.

The sergeant returned. 'The professor's finished and the Home Office bloke's packing up, sir. He said you wanted a word before he goes off.'

Hayes jumped up, making hasty farewells, promising to be in touch in the morning.

When they had gone the old couple eyed each other with renewed anxiety, recognizing that their quiet retirement in Didcot Drive was under serious threat.

'How about a proper drink, Meg? Open the duty free. We deserve a pick-me-up after all this.'

Five

The pathologist was waiting in the hall when Hayes hurried in.

'Sorry to have kept you, Dr James. Everything coming together?'

'More or less. Professor Glyn has gone back to Oxford with his little exhibits while I supervise the transfer of the corpse before our work begins. He will rejoin me for supper before we start on the post-mortem. We liaised on a research project some years ago and have kept in touch. Fascinating work! Glyn is one of the leading forensic entomologists in the country – we're lucky to have him more or less on the doorstep, as it were. He gives evidence both here and abroad, you know. Amazing chap.'

'Can't say I'd have much of an appetite for supper after what you two have been delving into this evening,' Hayes quipped.

'Once you get two scientists with a case like this, the interest blanks out the human aspect.'

'But maggots!' Hayes whistled. 'Blimey – it's enough to make you throw up even in my line of business. The poor woman must have lain here undiscovered for well over a week. Did the professor come to any initial conclusion?'

'Wouldn't commit himself – he has to confirm his first thoughts under the microscope, of course. But you're a lucky man, Chief Inspector. To have Glyn on the case is very fortunate, believe me.'

They moved back to the conservatory.

'Can you give me some clue about the actual killing?'

'I need to get the body on the bench for any definitive conclusions but it would seem that there are three wounds: one to the temple and one to the neck, but the most vicious jabs were to the thigh, possibly as she fell to the ground. It is likely that the victim bled to death. An untidy stabbing, in my opinion. Not the sort of attack one would expect from a man familiar with wielding a knife.'

Hayes winced. 'Not your average thug then?'

The doctor shrugged, but Hayes persisted.

'She didn't die immediately?'

'No.'

'Killed here, would you agree?'

'From the bloody smears on the floor tiles – your photographer took dozens of shots, by the way – I'd guess she was standing about here,' he said, pointing at the coffee table, 'fell, then crawled round the back of the sofa and died later.'

Hayes drew a sharp breath, calculating the ripples from this act of callous indifference. The murderer must have turned off the lights in here and bolted, leaving the woman gurgling in her own blood, unable to cry out and dying alone in the dark.

'What sort of weapon?'

'Obviously a short blade, but I will have to delve further on that one.'

The men arrived to bag up the body and place it in the waiting van. James issued curt demands, abandoning Hayes while this gruesome procedure was completed. He returned to pack his bag.

Hayes was intrigued by the situation the introduction of his colleague, the professor, presented.

'Tell me, doctor, what happens now?'

'The body is placed in the mortuary and I join Professor

Glyn there for an initial discussion on the procedure, thus leaving the scene of the crime clear for your team to continue their own investigations. It is customary to allow any forensic expert brought into the lab to make the first examination, as the pathologist's work could destroy details important to an entomologist for example. The professor will tape a commentary for the benefit of the police officers present and for future appraisal and a photographer is on hand to record important aspects of the autopsy.'

'And when will the results be known? I have quite a load on my hands, and attending the post-mortem will presumably take up considerable time.'

James looked at his watch. 'There is usually some delay at the mortuary. I doubt whether the work will begin until well after midnight.'

He buttoned his raincoat and after a further brief exchange left by the garden door and drove away.

Bellamy sidled up. 'Did the Robotham girl say whether the conservatory door was open, sir? The professor told me he'll need to know.'

'Difficult to get much sense out of her tonight. But find out, will you? Robbins might still be with her at her cottage. Ask her to check and let you know and you can leave a message at the mortuary. That new girl, Robbins, seems bright – know anything about her?'

'New girl, as you say, sir. Seems willing enough though. Came over from Thame with some others to help with a big push on car theft we had in the summer and got transferred to Renham when she got a share of a house, in this village as it happens. Sings in the choir, so I've heard.'

Hayes frowned. 'Sounds useful. I'd like Robbins on the A team – take her off her usual duties so she can concentrate on this. A nasty business, Roy.'

Bellamy blinked, wondering what had brought on Hayes'

sudden confidentiality which, so far, had slumbered underground even in their private conversations.

'Look, I could do with a sandwich or a take-away. Could you send out for something to eat all round? It looks like we've got a night's work ahead of us.'

After the body had been transferred to the mortuary van, Hayes took stock of the crime scene. The conservatory lighting had been augmented by auxiliary spotlights rigged up by the crime scene squad, and the place lay under illumination as stark as on a lab bench. Everything was remarkably undisturbed, no sign of a struggle and, apart from the broken glass crunching underfoot and dark areas of dried blood, it looked almost homely. Outside, two officers were scouring the garden.

A rattan sofa faced a pair of cane chairs across a bamboo coffee table, the cushions neatly in place, a red woollen 'throw' tumbled half under the couch, possibly dragged by the dying woman's efforts to stem the flow of blood. The blinds were drawn indicating a visitor after dark or perhaps some sort of heat conservation measure. A precaution against an October chill to protect the plants?

Hayes knew nothing about horticulture but, gazing round, he could not but marvel at the rows of orchids, bright as butterflies, ranged about the slatted shelving. In view of having been unattended for more than a week, the blooms showed no signs of neglect. But then the old boy next door had said something about a misting system, hadn't he? Hayes hoped that Fred Mason was going to help him out with more than village gossip before this case was solved.

He asked Bellamy to check out the garage but, just as the sergeant was leaving, called him back.

'Just one thing. Was the door leading from here into the house unlocked?'

'Oh yeah. And the fingerprint boys dusted right through. Plenty of dabs, they said, but if this Prentice woman did a bit of hairdressing in the conservatory, used it as a makeshift salon there would be, wouldn't there?'

'Ask around in the morning. We'll set up an extensive door-to-door. People who live in these culs-de-sac know everything that goes on, and with six houses looking in on each other and one attractive woman living on her own, curiosity kicks in immediately.'

'There's stacks of hairdressing stuff in the cupboard under the sink, guv. A pile of towels an' all, shower attachment in the sink, a plug for a hairdryer – it's all set up for the odd trim and blow-dry.'

'It's something we can look into, Roy. But the kid who found the body said something about the victim's customers being nursing home residents or house-bound people, so using her home facilities wouldn't necessarily register much extra income, would it? Maybe it was a come-on for her boyfriends. A head massage and a bit of personal attention for specials.'

Bellamy's mental picture of exotic goings-on amongst the orchids struck a chord and he stared round with enthusiasm.

'OK, let's get started. Get one of the constables to take notes while you see what the search team have found.'

Bellamy started to speak but Hayes had moved off, striding through the living room, casing the set-up with the cold eye of an estate agent. He started at the top, taking the stairs two at a time, following his nose straight to the bedroom which, from previous experience, was the focus of any woman's comfort zone, the place most likely to yield up secrets. His 'gofer', a plump young officer clearly anxious not to put a foot wrong with the new DCI, hovered in his wake, not altogether sure what was required of him.

Finding the diary was a bonus and with silent applause Hayes extracted it from its hidey-hole inside a hatbox stored high on top of the wardrobe.

Six

Hayes dictated some notes to the ruddy-faced constable and logged the diary into the investigation, grinning like a marathon runner rounding the first checkpoint.

He decided to put the case to bed for a few hours and, pocketing the diary, sauntered downstairs. He paused in the sitting room, surveying the set-up with renewed interest. Sandy Prentice had a certain style, he'd give her that: the room was lavishly furnished, pride of place given to a baby grand piano which dominated the low-ceilinged room. He touched the keyboard, then struck several chords, admiring the clear tone of the obviously expensive instrument. Sheet music jammed inside the bench seat suggested an eclectic taste, everything from pop to Schubert.

No framed photographs littered the mantelpiece and only one picture graced the walls, a modern limited edition print of a ballet dancer, cross-legged, tying the ribbons of her pumps. Pastel, predictable and pretty – pretty boring, Hayes concluded, but all of a piece with the buttoned chesterfield and repro Louis Something dining chairs. Roger Hayes was not into décor but fancied himself at pricing any item of furniture. After years wedded to Patsy and her passion for house makeovers, he had learned the hard way about furnishing a room with the latest thing.

The kitchen was immaculate but at first glance underused, the oven clean as a whistle and the fridge sporting little apart from a bottle of rancid milk and a freezer compartment with a small sliced loaf and two low-fat meals for one. The pantry was all but bare.

The lady eats out a lot, he concluded, wishing someone would get a move on with that sandwich he'd ordered half an hour ago. He made a swift recce of the other rooms, pausing in the television room, which featured a cosy velvet sofa for two, a glass topped coffee table and a bar well stocked with cocktail mixers. He almost missed the filing cabinet lurking behind the bar counter like a teetotaller at a party.

He went off to find the bunches of keys from the dead woman's handbag, all neatly bagged up and tagged for the police records. The filing cabinet comprised three drawers bulging with folders. Hayes sighed, assessing the hours of desk work involved in dissecting Sandy Prentice's tax returns, bank statements and business correspondence. There were no private letters, no *billets doux* of any kind and, to the casual observer, the obsessive filing system could only belong to a businesswoman with no love interest or family life of any kind, an impression clearly well off the mark as far as social engagements went, judging by the wardrobe full of elegant evening clothes and drawers overflowing with silk underwear of an alluring appeal that Hayes had never had the luck to admire on real women. The only nugget hidden amongst the dross was a stack of soft porn videos that no self-respecting teenager would blush over.

He relocked the cabinet and put off the book-keeping for later, wondering why this astute operator had never invested in a computer. Perhaps a laptop had gone missing? Could it be that the murderer, having stolen none of the valuable items here for the taking, was not a burglar after all but someone who had arrived with the clear intention of removing any whiff of a relationship with Sandy Prentice and had found himself unexpectedly confronted by the lady of the house? One of the scene-of-crime officers had mentioned that the lamps inside lit up each night on an automatic time switch at seven even when the occupier was at home, leaving any potential intruder with plenty of guesswork.

It was time to push off and, after instructing the officers still on site, he was unlocking his car as Bellamy hurried over with a take-away pizza carton.

'Yeah, well, thanks, but I'm off for now – I've got some reading to do.' He tapped the diary and they exchanged words about the next steps.

'One more thing, guv. Our victim ran a smashing car. MG ZT, a real goer, would have cost over twenty thousand new. All locked up but are the car keys still available?'

'With Sergeant Buller – tell him I said he's to give it a going over in the morning. No point in starting anything new tonight but see me tomorrow – eight sharp at the station, OK? Put the word round. I'd like to have a team briefing before everyone gets stuck in on their own line, especially the auxiliary men the Super's brought in. And I particularly want to talk to Robbins afterwards. Tell her I'm attaching her to my squad for this job. I'm going back now to check out some paperwork before I join the pathology team at the mortuary. Give me a call if anything breaks – the SOCO team is still picking over the scene. You'd better check with Superintendent Waller and find out if he wishes to join me at the post-mortem when it gets under way. Ask the mortuary attendant to give me a buzz on my mobile when they're ready to start.'

Bellamy nodded, far from sure that standing by a mortuary bench would do much for anyone's appetite.

Hayes decided to keep out of Waller's line of fire for a little longer and drove back to his flat in Haddenham, a small town with a railway link which could whisk him to London in fifty minutes which, with his limited free time, struck him as being a good alternative to driving.

Roger Hayes was a music buff, a passion he could now

indulge without moans and groans from Patsy, whose preference had been for movies and clubbing. He was starting to enjoy this newfound freedom of choice and since the divorce had also launched into increasingly confident duets with a wok and a wickedly lethal Japanese meat cleaver.

His new flat comprised four rooms over a butcher's shop. It overlooked the village pond, the quarrelsome quacking of the ducks an unavoidable wake-up call. The place suited him, its sparse interior barely furnished by normal standards, though hardly the sort of thing Patsy derided as 'minimalist tat'. In fact, the women he had occasionally invited to share his king-size bed had no complaints. The tall detective with the broken nose and boot-black crewcut was, after all, not nearly as formidable as at first glance, a wry sense of humour breaking through after the first glass of wine. And the butcher certainly liked his new tenant, anticipating no trouble with the inevitable Christmas break-ins since a fully-fledged copper moved on to the premises to keep an eye on the turkeys.

Hayes had a shower, warmed up the pizza and settled with a glass of Beaujolais to sift through Sandy Prentice's diary.

Seven

The diary was a disappointment. He had hoped for heart-felt confessions, secret liaisons, anything in fact to point the way to Sandy's life outside the cul-de-sac in Newton Greys.

It was, in effect, an engagement diary, a detailed timesheet of the contract work with various chi-chi clinics and nursing homes which were known, even to Hayes, from snippets in the tabloids. It was interesting that Sandy had clearly kept any gossip about the glitzier establishments to herself, neither Meg Mason, her neighbour, nor Melanie Crabbe, her cleaner, mentioning the fact she worked with anyone other than elderly people. If they had known about these other, classier treatment centres this titillating piece of information would certainly have come up. Wouldn't it? One, a psychiatric clinic in Aylesbury, specialized in discreet detox for models and pop stars, and drying-out sessions for stressed-out politicians, plus the bread and butter medical treatment of wealthy clients who paid for privacy. It was a lucrative market but surely, as a hairdresser, even as a snipper to the stars, Sandy Prentice could hardly make the sort of money that his glance through her bank statements had indicated? But who was he to know about the rewards in the beauty lark, a man who balked at spending a tenner at his local barber's? He wondered why she thought it necessary to hide the diary in a hatbox.

After the initial discouragement, he set to with a notebook to list the relevant addresses. Checking with Sandy's employers would be a start. On closer examination there were also nebulous references to bookings nearer home and, intriguingly, a page of telephone numbers linked merely with initials.

He decided to put WDC Robbins on to it, get her to check them out: four at least were recognizable from dialling codes as being local.

He scrolled through the diary more closely, calculating the regular bookings Sandy undertook and working out a rough schedule for a lady who drove up in style in her own MG.

I bet that put the nurses' noses out of joint, he thought, picturing the flamboyant arrival of the crimper whose charm, if Meg Mason's assurances were to be believed, was probably more than half the appeal to the depressed patients in their enforced 'cold turkey'.

He packed up the diary and notebook and glanced at his watch. Well after midnight, by God. And tomorrow would be even worse. Even so, his pulse quickened at the complexities of his first murder investigation since arriving at Renham. Stroke of luck, that. A mysterious single woman struck down in her own home, dying by degrees from blood loss, the body lying in a swiftly decomposing state in a bower of orchids: all the makings of a real headliner. He drove to the mortuary to attend the autopsy, wondering if the Prentice case would turn out to be his lucky break or yet another stumbling block.

Next morning he assembled his team at the station, putting Bellamy in charge of co-ordinating results, and marking the card of a trio of known backsliders all too keen to dodge the routine house-to-house enquiries that inevitably burdened any serious case.

Hayes regarded the assorted officers at his disposal, all

too well aware that his standing as the new man on the beat had yet to make him either friends or foes. His manner was affable but steely-eyed, his rapport limited so far to Sergeant Bellamy, fiftyish and a stickler for paperwork, and another older officer, Buller, who he was assured would be the right man to join the car mechanics to go over the MG. On a hunch, the new girl, Jenny Robbins, who lived in Newton Greys, seemed useful and looked just the sort to elicit confidences from the neighbours.

She sat at the back, clearly embarrassed by the ribbing from her mates, whose barbed jokes hinted that the pretty constable with the long auburn hair and long legs to match was likely to leapfrog promotion if she played her cards right.

After a short briefing Hayes compounded matters by asking her to stay behind. They moved into his office and he closed the door, seating himself at the desk, leaving the girl to find herself a chair and bring it forward.

'Now, constable. This is your first murder investigation I take it?'

'I was attached to a team looking into that killing of an undergraduate at St Ildica's a couple of years ago.'

'Ah, yes, the boyfriend hid the body under the floorboards I seem to remember.'

She nodded.

'Nothing else?'

'I've only been on the force for four years,' she snapped.

Hayes smiled, recognizing a spark of redhead temper under the professional air.

'I'm new here myself,' he said with a grin. 'So we're quits, OK? Now, here's the agenda. I want you to get straight back to Newton Greys and do a cheek-to-cheek with that poor girl who found the body. Mrs – er, no, – Miss – Robotham. You met the mother when you took her home last night?'

'Yes. Both are locals, born in the village. The mother works up at Kelvin Court. Does cleaning for Lady Honora. She's been on the staff for years. Lives on the estate.'

'But the daughter's got her own place in the village. Sounds pretty cushy. Single mother, I presume. Partner?'

'No man on the scene as far as I could see. There's a little boy about six or seven who goes to school in the village. Tansy rents the cottage from Major Vennor at the Court. Presumably her mother's influence with Lady Honora persuaded him to let Tansy have an estate cottage on special terms. She works at Kelvin Court with Robotham Senior part-time and does the cosmetics lark as an extra.'

'Well done. You managed to get her to open up, then, when she got home? She was pretty hysterical before, as you saw. I want you to get a signed statement this morning. I expect the mother's staying on till the girl gets over the shock. Encourage any loose talk about the deceased – every little helps.'

'Yes, sir. Actually the mother's the chatty one.'

'And when you've milked that situation perhaps you would check out these telephone numbers,' he said, passing over a list of the numbers copied from Sandy's engagement diary. 'No need to introduce yourself, an anonymous caller getting the wrong number, eh? I just want to know who these telephone numbers belong to. Use the usual police channels as a last resort – a couple of the numbers are mobiles. Just keep your cool, Robbins, we don't want to frighten any contacts. Get me? Word travels like wildfire in a village and I don't want any of her clients put on the defensive before I get to talk to them.'

She pushed the list into her pocket and half rose, but he hadn't finished with her yet and irritably waved at her to sit down.

'And fit in a chat with the local newsagent at the post office; it's a general store, they do newspapers.'

'Yes, I know it.'

'Right. Flash your ID and ask when he delivered the magazine to number six. I want to know how long it has been poking out of the door and did the Prentice woman always say when she'd be away? Speak to the paper boy – he may have seen something.'

'OK. That all, sir?'

'Then join up with Sergeant Bellamy on his rounds in Didcot Drive. Can't believe that new neighbours living cheek by jowl in a cul-de-sac can't fill in some gaps on our victim. I haven't found a photograph of her so far but I got the impression she was still a looker, though the mortuary slab didn't do her any favours last night. Check at her house, see if anything useful in the way of recent snaps of the deceased have turned up. Holiday snaps? Boyfriends? Use your loaf, Robbins.'

'Am I to report directly to you, sir?'

'Type a full report and give it to Bellamy. He's co-ordinating the information as it comes in. I'm off to Oxford this morning to see our forensic entomologist, Professor Glyn. And don't forget, as I said at the briefing, I don't want any comment whatsoever about the maggots – it's just the thing to bring the media down around our necks and I'd like to keep our investigation as low key as possible. Do I make myself clear? Impress on the Robotham women that gossiping about the state of the dead woman's body is a serious offence. Lay it on thick. Scare the living daylights out of them if necessary.' He shuffled his papers and rose, dismissing the girl with a curt nod.

She paused at the door.

'Do I get transport, sir?'

'Be nice to Sergeant Buller, see what he's got free. Say I gave the OK. Otherwise you'll have to get a lift from one of the others and leg it once they drop you off at Newton Greys.'

She closed the door, mentally gauging the reaction of the rest of the station if she did manage to nab so much as a runabout from 'Uncle' Buller.

Eight

Professor Glyn's office occupied space carved from a biology lab which was part of a modern science block largely paid for by a generous donation from Sir Walter Tongue, an arms dealer wishing to enhance his reputation with those opposed to wealth generated by guns and bullets.

Roger Hayes held no strong political views, his off-duty hours taken up by scrambled efforts to salvage a diminishing musicianship. As a student he had harboured serious ambitions to train as a classical pianist but, life being the bitch that it is, his dreams of a career on the concert platform were icily cut short by the unassailable opinion of his tutor that 'Roger, you've got talent, no doubt about that, but I'm afraid not enough to endure the disappointment. Think of something else, dear boy.'

It was a devastating blow. Roger Hayes, aged twenty-two, jumped disastrously into marriage and for no good reason joined the police. The first decision had proved a mistake, the second, to his surprise, a challenge he grew to relish.

The professor looked up wearily from his desk, eyeing the dark haired, vaguely familiar figure blocking his doorway with a blank stare. Obviously not a research student, he decided, too old and too neatly turned out, but the lean features suddenly came into focus. He jumped up, holding out his hand, smiling apologetically.

'Ah, Inspector, or is it Chief Inspector? I am constantly

in the doghouse here for omitting distinctions in rank – so important at Oxford, as you well know.'

'Professor Glyn. It is good of you to see me so early – I gather you had a long night of it at the mortuary.'

'Please, make yourself comfortable. Roger Hayes, isn't it? Let's ditch the formalities, shall we? Life's too short. Hector James spoke well of you. Call me George, everyone here does.'

In daylight and divested of his professional protective clothing, the entomologist with the formidable reputation was a stout figure, probably more than fifty-five, but with the twinkling eyes of a natural enthusiast. He wore a grey polo-neck sweater under a tweed suit, and as he hurriedly rounded the desk to shake hands and to draw up a chair for Hayes he sent an overflowing ashtray spinning to the floor, spreading ash and cigarette butts across the carpet. He replaced the ashtray and rang for his secretary. A frizzy haired girl in denims appeared, looking distinctly sulky.

'Fran, my dear, have you finished typing up my notes from last night? Bring them in, would you, sweetie? The Chief Inspector is in a hurry.'

She exited with a flourish.

Glyn turned to Hayes and murmured, 'These girls come and go – I hardly learn their names before they're off again, poached by those wretched research Fellows who seem to have no more success than I at keeping even one decent typist.'

She returned, placed a folder on the desk and swept out with the dignity of a princess – which, in fact, in the sellers' market for pretty PAs, she was.

'I expect your requirements are specialized, George,' said Hayes. 'Girls gravitate to Oxford thinking it's all May Balls and a surplus of nice young men, and forget it's got a life of its own apart from the university, a motor industry of sorts at least.'

'My work is far from thrilling to these girls, of course.

Maggots? Insects? Dreary data with unceasing recourse to a specialized glossary of scientific terms. Hardly glamorous.'

Hayes leaned forward, eager to jump the gun with the forensic report, to be in at the kill, to put it bluntly. 'Did you establish a time of death, George?'

'Ah, yes, the crucial question. May I illustrate my conclusions?'

He opened a refrigerator tucked away in the corner of the room and placed a row of lidded dishes on the edge of the desk.

'These little fellows,' he said with all seriousness, 'are the most important witnesses you are likely to have.'

Hayes tensed, eyeing the tiny specimens with interest.

'This species – I won't bore you with scientific terms which you can read in my report – are known to breed late in the season and therefore their existence in October is not rare. The environment was unusual, of course: a heated greenhouse in effect, a place with organic matter readily available and an unwilling host to these little flies in the form of a bleeding body lying under the staging with her head half in the soil of the lower bed.'

'She was found behind the sofa, George.'

'Indeed so. But my colleague contributed valuable facts on that score. Matching soil samples were found in the victim's hair, and a trail of bloodstains leads us to the conclusion that the poor lady dragged herself along the floor.'

'The flies attacked her wounds while she was alive?'

'Doubtful, but the attraction would have been instantly registered and these flies don't waste much time with a host to hand. I examined pupal cases under the electron microscope and these small insects, a form of dung fly, were breeding profusely, leading me to conclude after a calculation of the life cycle that the lady was stabbed on Thursday the fourth of October. She died no more than two hours later, according to the pathologist's estimation.'

'The development of the maggots can establish that she died that day?'

'Probably later that day, in the afternoon or early evening, but before the sun had gone down. Here, let me give you my report to study at your leisure. If you have any questions, please do not hesitate to call me.'

'You are willing to give evidence?'

'But of course. I shall keep my specimens here if you don't mind. Under laboratory conditions. It has been known,' he added with a wry smile, 'for evidence to go missing or to be defiled in police custody, has it not?'

He stood, grinning like a rotund Buddha, holding out the slim folder to Hayes. They shook hands and the professor politely walked him down to the main entrance.

'The pathologist has the bulk of the evidence, of course. We drew some interesting conclusions from the autopsy which he will elaborate for you. My own contribution was a small one, Roger. I have no wish to put my old friend Hector's investigations in the shade with my little dung flies.'

Hayes glanced at the report as he sat in the car, realizing that the scientific evidence would be crucial. It was also apparent that the delay in the discovery of the body would complicate the investigation to no small degree, the recollections of possible witnesses inevitably clouded by the passage of time.

He drove off at speed, anxious to get back to the murder scene and see if the SOCO team had come up with anything interesting. Stopping at a set of traffic lights, he scanned a billboard advertising the appearance of Florian Brandt at the Music Festival later that month. The young tenor was establishing a reputation of note and Hayes, hoping to get lucky, had already booked two tickets for his subsequent recital at the Wigmore Hall in November, although persuading one of the current girlfriends to join him seemed as unlikely as closing the Prentice case down by then.

He sighed, knowing all too well that the chances of catching Brandt at this Oxford preview would also, in view of the urgency of the investigation, be far from likely – unless, that was, an unexpected breakthrough tied up the case in days.

'Fat chance,' he muttered, clashing the gears, but, ever the optimist, he stopped off at the festival box office and bought himself a ticket.

Nine

Hayes bought a sandwich and some petrol at the filling station. The sky was now overcast, threatening rain, and it felt to him as if the day was already ebbing away, leaking precious hours and shortening the time in which he could usefully get on with sifting the evidence.

He called in to find out whether there had been any new developments while he had been in Oxford. Bellamy tried to sound hopeful.

'Nothing much, guv, but everyone's still at it, asking round the village, doing the usual. Sergeant Buller and the police mechanic from Thame've been pulling the MG apart but nothing's turned up. Nearly new vehicle, perfectly kosher, supplied eight months ago by a garage in south London, paid for in cash.'

'Whew!'

'Yeah, right. Buller and the engineer went down the pub in Newton Greys for a pint and a wad after, and propped up the bar, which was all fired up with the crime.'

'Anything useful? No, don't bother – I'll get it from Buller later. I want to get back to the village straight away. Who's still there?'

'A couple of uniformed men. The SOCO team's packed it in but Frame, the local bobby, is holding the fort and I'll get back as soon as I've squared up the reports from the door-to-door squad.'

Hayes drove off at speed, keen to waste no more time

faffing about with the paperwork. The rain set in in earnest, only the constable on the gate at number 6 and a police car parked outside giving any sign of trouble. No curtains twitched as Hayes drew up but he had the distinct impression of being observed. Unnerving. He ran through the rain and into the house, where Jenny Robbins was seated at the dining table, bashing away at a portable typewriter. She jumped up as he entered, green eyed as an alley cat.

'Afternoon, sir. Just finishing my notes on the door-to-door.'

'And?'

'Nothing much. The Masons were the most co-operative, but the people at number four and two are working couples so I'll have to catch them later. There's another retired couple living directly opposite here at number one, the Harrises and—'

'With the cat.'

'Eh?'

'Never mind. Just get on with it, will you?'

'Well, as I was about to say, Mrs Harris was the one who put the magazine through the letterbox. I spoke to the newsagent and he remembered there was a bit of a blistering from her about his paper boy. It appears Mrs Harris is constantly complaining about late delivery of their *Guardian* and the kid often mixes up the orders, says the marking-up's hard to read now it's darker in the mornings. Anyway, the magazine went to the wrong house and Mrs Harris went back to the shop and played hell with the owner.'

'Bit over the top, wasn't it? Not far, is it? The village shop I presume.'

She nodded. 'Well, I called to see the Harris woman myself,' she said, grinning, 'and she seemed as incensed by the nature of the magazine as anything else. Had a raunchy front cover and was, as she called it, "a disgusting rag, clearly not the sort of thing either Mr Harris or myself would read, and embarrassing that the neighbours in the Drive would assume we did, the thing spread out by the gate for everyone to see".'

'Not through the door?'

'The Harrises have a special letterbox nailed to the gate – they've got a nasty little dog and prefer the postman and newsboy to keep out. But the Prentice woman's magazine was too bulky so the boy left it on top in full view. After a bollocking aimed at the boy, she said, she told the newsagent she'd deliver it herself as Mrs Prentice only lived opposite, and she popped it through the door a week ago.'

'Thought nothing of leaving a clear indication that the occupier was away then?'

Robbins shrugged. 'There's not much Neighbourhood Watch mentality round here, sir. And I got the impression that Sandy Prentice's choice of reading matter was not the only thing Mrs Harris disapproved of. I guess she hoped to get a peek inside number six when she called round, nosy old bag. I can't see her offering to do the paper boy's job as a neighbourly gesture. Apparently the Harrises were away at Christmas so missed the chance when Sandy invited the locals in for a drinks party.'

'Sounds promising. I think I'll have a word with this *Guardian*-reading gorgon myself – nothing like a spiteful neighbour for filling in the gaps. Are the Harrises the only retired people in the road apart from the Masons?'

'Yes. There's a young woman with a baby at number two next to the Harris couple but she's only been living there since July so wasn't much help.'

'I thought these houses were new?'

'Yeah, well, I asked her about that. It seems the original owners had a running battle with Mr Harris about the boundary fence, got fed up and sold up. The new people seem to have had no trouble.'

Hayes laughed. 'Not yet! It beats me, this business about rows over the garden fence. I read in the paper last week about one poor bloke getting shot over his cat fouling the neighbour's vegetable patch. I thought this village counted as "rural", you wouldn't expect these suburban confrontations about boundary lines and the fecklessness of a spotty paper boy.'

He moved off, chuckling, leaving Robbins to her report.

The conservatory had been well and truly picked over, and the throw had disappeared, together with several items for forensic examination which the Home Office pathologist had requested. The broken glass had been swept up and the sofa pulled up to the low table just as, he imagined, the poor dead woman would have wished.

Hayes crossed to the garden door and gazed out at the rain. The cul-de-sac had been developed from a piece of land adjoining a stubble field, a barn of sorts commanding the far side of the field, which was bisected by a footpath, presumably a public right of way connecting the eastern edge of the village to the church. He called through to Robbins, who skittered in to join him, coltish in brown leather trousers and a yellow jumper.

'Sir?'

'You live in this village, I gather.'

'In Church Lane.'

'Here, draw me a rough map, would you? And where does that footpath out there lead to?'

She fetched a shorthand notebook and they sat on the sofa in the conservatory like a pair of ramblers planning a hike.

'The oldest part of the village is set round the church but the centre has grown away over the years,' she said, sketching a network of streets bisected by a straight modern road on which the pub and the general store-cum-post office were situated. 'Low Road runs south, linking the main road to Kelvin Court, and Church Lane, see, this bit here, skirts the Old Rectory and a row of cottages backed by the council estate.'

'All densely developed I see.'

She nodded. 'The primary school is opposite the church and has about sixty kids I'm told. There's always a threat of it closing down and the council bussing the children to Renham. The public footpath out there you were asking about crosses the field and comes out on the main road but then continues across another field and is used as a short cut to the church and the school. Parents use it in the summer but take their cars when the weather's bad even though it's only half a mile beyond the centre. Then there's a council estate on the other side of Low Road where Tansy Robotham lives. The cottages on that side are part of the Kelvin Court estate and are mostly occupied by farmworkers. The bigwig around here is Major Vennor from the Court, who sold this site to the builders to put up Didcot Drive plus a bigger development of "executive homes" as they call them, which skirts the bridleway all the fuss was about last year. You wouldn't have taken much interest in it, sir, but the squire's efforts to stop ramblers crossing his land created a big bust-up in the village, everyone taking sides, not always for decent reasons. Vennor came in for a lot of flak when he sold off the land for new housing which was too expensive for the locals and brought in a crowd of outsiders who, it was said, would contribute nothing to the village and would make the place a suburban outpost for commuters.'

'Oh, the joys of country living!' Hayes grinned and, taking the notebook from her, tore out the page and slipped it into his pocket.

'Thanks, Robbins. Keep your ear to the ground, will you? I expect the locals will be more than a little anxious till we catch the killer. No joke having a man with a knife at large.'

'You think he's local?'

'Might be. Though Mrs Prentice seemed to have a full life one way and another. Listen out if you hear of anyone who had private hairdos in her conservatory. Especially any men. Oh, and by the way, this vicar . . . what was his name again?'

'Harcourt. Lives in the new vicarage next to the church. Calls himself Father Peter. Unmarried which is just as well as he's lumbered with three parishes so doesn't have much time for pints in the local, even on quiz nights.'

'You don't like him?'

'Oh, he's OK. Means well but he's a bit of a red. Bangs on in the pulpit about foreign debt in the Third World and so on, which doesn't interest the congregation much and gets him no Brownie points with Major Vennor, who's very touchy about people owing money, some say because his no-good sons fritter it away on the horses. He used to pay for a lot of local amenities, donated the site for the new village hall for starters and set up his wife as chairman of the Village Hall Committee. But after a couple of run-ins with the vicar she chucked it in and the new woman in charge has pushed her way in, a Mrs Chambers, considered a bit of a "nouveau" by the rest apparently but she's throwing money at all sorts of projects in the village, so they turn a blind eye to her taking over from Lady Honora, who is a nice old duck and not at all pushy.' She paused, sensing that Hayes was becoming impatient. 'But that's another story.'

'Right.' Hayes gazed round at the banked tiers of pot plants. 'Nip next door to the Masons, would you? Ask – very politely, mind – if Mr Mason would be good enough to step in here for a quick word.'

Ten

When Robbins had gone, Hayes found himself alone in the house for the first time, standing in the dead woman's living room, an interloper, an uninvited stranger here to unpick her life, to infiltrate her every personal possession. This feeling had never hampered his professional life before and it was not as if the object of his scrutiny was likely to have been the least bit appealing to him in life.

He gazed round the sitting room, its obvious femininity nauseating as saccharine, the only dissonant note the solidity of the Steinway, which took up far too much space and which, on reflection, seemed incongruous. Why would a woman such as Sandy Prentice choose such a macho object of desire? And glossy black too. A stab of envy was quickly brushed aside. Hayes could picture the occupier of this cosy ambiance buying a white piano – or even an upright, a neat Japanese job that would never have the audacity to dominate the room as this one did.

It was not as if the wretched victim had been really talented, was it? Vamping away at the vicar's summer concert was hardly the slot for a determined virtuoso, one would have thought. But what did he know, he who had not touched a keyboard in years, tormented by the knowledge that his own technique was irretrievably flawed, and too proud to enjoy a bit of harmless tinkling like the sad creature who now lay on a mortuary slab?

Frame, the local PC, now firmly located at the door of number 6 burst in, his face aglow, the very picture of the village bobby.

'Excuse me, sir, but there's a message from the station. The lady's solicitor, Mr Hardcastle, wants to see you urgently. He's worried about the security of his client's property, apparently.'

Hayes' laugh was bitter. 'What? With coppers on the door day and night? Does he think we're making away with the teabags?'

Frame looked anxious, but persisted. 'Shall I tell them to send him over?'

'No. He'll have to make an appointment and come to the station. Say I'll phone him back.'

Frame turned to go, colliding in the hall with a skinny kid who had slipped through the front door while the coast was apparently clear.

'Hey, you! Stop there, miss. You can't come in here. Oh, it's you, Melanie. Well, just push off, this is no place for you.' He raised both arms as if he was herding a recalcitrant heifer back into the field. Hayes stepped forward.

'Wait. Are you the cleaner?'

'It's Melanie Crabbe, sir,' Frame put in, caught between these two determined characters like a landlord anticipating a pub brawl.

The girl could hardly have weighed eight stone, her scrawny arms jerking from the sleeves of a man's outsize sweatshirt as if to fend off the hapless Frame.

'I've only come for my stuff, Gary Frame, so don't you try pushing me around, see.'

Hayes waved her inside, nodding to Frame, who reluctantly withdrew.

'OK. Now, what is it you want?'

'Just me slippers and me overall. I leave them here in the broom cupboard and now Sandy don't need me no more,

I thought I'd better get me stuff before the place gets all locked up.'

'You took a chance, didn't you? Barging in here past a police cordon just to pick up a couple of bits. Come off it, Melanie, what's your game?'

Her eyes narrowed.'What's it to you?'

Hayes grinned. 'Cheeky little bird, aren't you? Clearly not frightened of a mere inspector then. Now, do we go down the nick for a formal interview or are you going to tell me what you really came for?'

She drew a packet of cigarettes from her jeans and lit up, sizing up Hayes with hard little eyes all but obscured by a ragged fringe bravely striped with maroon highlights. Multiple gold rings pierced her pretty ears.

'Yeah, well, Sandy used to stash me wages in a coffee jar in the kitchen.'

'Even if you didn't work? She didn't give you a key, did she, Mel? If she was off working on your Wednesday you got paid anyway?'

'Yeah, sometimes she left a note at the pub – I do washing up nights – for me to turn up another morning but mostly I just had to take it as it come. Leave me a key?' she said with a guffaw. 'That bloody woman wouldn't even let me in the back door. "You just ring the bell, Melanie," she'd say, "and if I'm not at home then it's your lucky day."'

'Sounds generous.'

Mel drew on her cigarette, her nails bitten to the quick. 'Well, that's what you think. Truth was, she thought I might help myself to some of that pile of make-up she keeps in her dressing table if I had a fucking key. Blimey, enough paint in there to give the royal yacht a second coat.'

'Maybe she just wanted to give Tansy Robotham a boost with her little cosmetics-to-go sideline.'

'Sandy? No way. Desperate, she was. Try anything to cover up the "laughter lines" as she called 'em.'

'Did she tell you she was going to be away?'

'No, she didn't. I turned up the next Wednesday as usual and I could see she weren't in. I kept an eye out but her magazine was still poking out the door days later.'

'Nobody else say anything about Sandy not being seen around?'

'Why should they? She was up and away all the bloody time and as her lights come on with the timeswitch who's to tell – or care, come to that?'

'She didn't have a special friend in the village you knew about?'

Melanie screwed up her mouth, the thin lips forming a tight little bud of indecision. 'We wasn't blabbing away like best mates. If there was a bloke or two it was all gossip, no one caught her at it, like. Apart from that piano tuner, course. He was flavour of the month all right, in an' out of this place like nobody's business.'

Hayes' voice sharpened. 'Why was that?'

'Trouble with that piano of hers. It was second-hand apparently. He got it for her through the trade but he kept having to come back to sort it out.'

'What was his name?'

'Johnny. That's what she called him. Nice-looking fella, younger than her, had a nice van an' all. Could have fancied him meself if it wasn't for the limp.'

'Bad?'

'No, not like a cripple but he hopped a bit and wore clumpy boots – p'raps one leg was shorter than the other or sommink. Don't ask me.'

'He lives in the village, this piano tuner?'

'No, said he come from Oxford when I give 'im a cup of coffee one time. Nice polite bloke, not like some.'

Hayes tried to recall the entries in the engagement diary; a visiting piano tuner wouldn't be hard to trace. 'Nothing else to cough up while we're being so chummy, Melanie?

I'd hate to find out you were holding out on me. Any coke, or Es, stashed away here you might find marketable at the pub on Saturday nights for instance?'

Mel walked away and stubbed out her cigarette on the base of a china figurine on the mantelshelf. She turned back, crossing her arms and giving Hayes the full force of her pinched gaze.

'If she did have anything to trade I'd be the last to find out, Inspector Know-all. Sandy Prentice played it close to her chest and all this,' she said, waving a hand dismissively, 'wasn't bought with hairdresser's tips, believe me.'

She shoved past and he followed her into the utility room, where she retrieved a nylon overall and a pair of scuffed slippers from the broom cupboard. She rolled them into a ball and headed for the door. Hayes blocked her exit.

'You never came in through the conservatory then, Melanie? Always rang at the doorbell, you said. Why was that?'

She shrugged. 'Gave her a chance to get her stuff together, I s'pose. Didn't want me to catch her doing summat she shouldn't.'

'Such as?'

'How would I know?'

Her look was direct but Hayes had dealt with dozens of hard-faced adolescents like Melanie Crabbe and decided to play Nice Cop for a bit.

'Well, that's fair enough. Thanks, Mel, I'll see you around. Tell you what, I'll ask the solicitor to make up your wages when he tots up the expenses, shall I? A fortnight owing, wasn't it? Four quid an hour, or shall we make it five?'

She shot a nervous look at the silhouette of Frame outside the front door and nodded dumbly, for a moment unsure of her footing.

'Sure, why not? Anything else?'

'When was the last time you cleaned up here?'

'Oh, that's easy – the Wednesday before last, the day before Jason's birthday. I needed the dosh to top up to buy him a proper pair of biker's boots.'

'I want you to come with me and have a very careful look round. See if anything's missing – anything strikes you as out of place. Got it?'

He led her through the house, insisting she took her time, confident of those darting black eyes of hers. But there was nothing; only the fridge caused her to pause.

'The champagne's gone. I clocked it meself when I was making a cup of tea. Socking great bottle of Bollinger. I seen pricy booze like that at the pub, but Mollie only gets it in on special order, for wedding anniversary bookings an' that. Mollie does a bit of catering on the side, three tables in the back room for the B&Bs.'

'Right.' He looked down at her trainers. 'Why the slippers, Mel? You don't strike me as a slippers girl. Heavy-footed, are you? Thumping about upstairs interrupting Sandy's piano practice.'

'Oh, it weren't just me. Sandy had a thing about her white carpets. Everyone had to wipe their shoes like they'd been shuffling through dogshit. If anyone come in by the garden door she made him take them off, even the piano tuner bloke. Got them to leave them on the mat like some sort of holy temple. Lived in fear and dread of mud on the rugs, that woman.'

'What, everyone?'

'Well, not the friends who come through the front door, just the people who come through the garden, see.' Except me. She hated my dirty trainers.

He let her into the hall and opened the front door, and Frame moved aside to let her pass. They watched her strut to the gate, her thin buttocks barely discernible in the tight blue jeans.

'Funny kid, that. You do know her address, Frame?'

'All too well, sir. Mel and that boyfriend of hers are always in trouble with the neighbours. Loud music, brawling, the usual "domestic", not to mention him revving up his motorbike at all hours, waking every kid in the village.'

Hayes grinned. 'I get the picture. As a matter of fact I quite took to her; a sparky little number like Melanie Crabbe might be useful. She works at the pub in the village, she said. Washing up.'

'So I heard. Lives with her grandad, old Mr Crabbe who used to do bike repairs and sell second-hand. Nice old bloke but disabled now, can't get out much. Melanie jumped in to look after him, "Saved me from the workhouse," he says. He gets on fine with the boyfriend but this one won't last. Our Melanie's fickle. They used to call her the "village bike" which wasn't fair – she's one of them silly girls who picks the rough but in the end gets tired of being the only one to bring in the wages.'

'There's something else, Frame. Did anyone empty the dustbin?'

'The SOCO team had it all out, sir. You could check with them.'

'Oh, and by the way, is there a recycling centre in the village? For papers, bottles, you know.'

'Yes, outside the village hall. See all the old biddies trying to put their cheap sherry bottles in the bin after dark, hoping no one's counting their empties.'

'Well, get on the blower and get the chap in charge to transport the bottle bin down to the depot so a couple of the lads can sift through for a likely murder weapon. I'm interested in a missing Bollinger champagne empty – it might be broken. And find out when the recycling bins were last emptied, will you? Don't look so glum, Frame, picking through broken glass isn't the worst job, is it? How about the poor sods who had to shovel up the maggots?'

Frame sketched a salute as Hayes moved back into the house just as Frederick Mason pushed open the gate and hurried inside in the wake of the tall inspector with the spiky manner who seemed to be in charge of this awful thing.

Eleven

'Ah, Mr Mason. Good of you to pop round. Come through to the conservatory, would you?'

The old man looked haunted, snatching a quick glance around the restored murder scene as if expecting blood to ooze freshly from the stained floor tiles.

'Take a seat.'

'No thanks. I'd best be getting back, Meg'll need some help stringing the onions.'

'Your own crop?'

'Yes. I've got an allotment next to the church for our veg. Keeps me out from under the wife's feet, you know.'

Hayes smiled and quickly got down to business.

'One or two small points you may be able to help me with, Mr Mason. The forensic team have recorded muddy footprints in here, local clay matching up to the field out there.' He pointed to the footpath bisecting the stubble field. 'Perhaps you use it yourself? Walking the dog, eh?'

'Course I do. It's the quickest way to the allotment.'

'The night you found poor Tansy here after she discovered the body . . . it was a damp evening. Did you cross the field, get your boots muddy?'

The old man looked alarmed, and Hayes swiftly intervened.

'Just an elimination enquiry, nothing to worry you, Mr Mason. It's just that I've been told Sandy was fussy about dirt tramping through the house and insisted people dumped their shoes before going through.'

'Yes, that's right. But that was only the workmen, painters and so on. Me, I always slipped off my wellingtons before coming in here to check the orchids but, in the normal way, Sandy wasn't house-proud with friends, not at all.'

'But on that night obviously you would have been too alarmed to bother about your boots, Tansy screaming her head off like you said.'

Mason nodded.

Hayes continued, choosing his words carefully. 'One of my officers will want to check your footwear, Mr Mason, to compare it with these footprints the forensic people are bothered about. We have to follow every lead, sir, however flimsy it may be.'

'Right. No problem. I'll warn Meg though: she's been sleeping badly since all this, wouldn't want her to start worrying about yours truly being a suspect, would we?' he added, with a wobbly attempt at a smile.

'Great. That's that then. Just one more thing. You did say Mrs Prentice employed a gardener.'

'That's right. Jim Loxley. But he wasn't a real gardener, he just cut the grass. Sandy did the weeding and planting out herself.'

Hayes made a note. 'You wouldn't know how I could reach Mr Loxley?'

'The people at number three get Jim over every week, they'd know. He also tidies up the shrubbery once or twice a year, that bit of rough ground in the middle of the cul-de-sac. I think the council pay him to do that, not that he's done a good job of it if you ask me. Those elderberries have gone wild this summer, need proper pruning though I wouldn't say no if they got cut down altogether. It's like a jungle; the kids from next door play Cowboys and Indians in there and with all this crime about, any mugger could hide in those bushes and jump out on anyone taking a stroll past.'

This little outburst had blown away Fred Mason's persistent anxiety and he drew Hayes aside to admire a spectacular slipper orchid blooming its heart out.

'See this, Chief Inspector? Lovely thing. Not as hardy as the cymbidiums but in the right conditions flowers for weeks on end. Would it be all right if I opened up the blinds?'

'Don't see why not. But tell me, are they normally like this?'

'Oh no. Sandy kept them open even at this time of the year. Didn't seem to bother about people looking in as they crossed the field. The orchids came first with the poor lady, they need a shaded light, see, and these louvred blinds are just the job.' He adjusted the blinds.

'At night too?'

'Oh yes. The temperature in here's pretty constant so long as the garden door's kept shut and they're not as fussy as people think. Been coping on their own while Meg and I have been away, haven't they? Goes to show, doesn't it?' He sighed. 'But whatever's going to happen to them after this, I ask myself?'

'Mrs Prentice's solicitor will probably have the answer to that. If I hear anything I'll let you know but I'm sure there would be no objection to you keeping an eye on the plants till the house is sold. I'll speak to Mr Hardcastle, shall I? Once we've finished up here ourselves the place will belong to whoever inherits. Mrs Prentice never mentioned any next-of-kin to you, did she?'

Mr Mason shook his head and moved away, his awareness of the bad vibrations of the place reasserting itself.

'But you and your wife are happy here?'

Mason paused, his rheumy eyes red-rimmed. 'Only one thing. The birds. Funny that. Before we came here we lived in Birmingham, bang in the centre, buildings all round. We retired to the country, thinking we'd enjoy the wildlife. But, do you know, there are no birds coming to the birdtable like in that scrubby bit of yard we had in the city? Hardly so much as a sparrow, and it's not as if there are any cats in the cul-de-sac apart from the Harrises' moggy across the road, and I've never seen it stir further than that wilderness in the middle of the run-round. Why do you think that is?'

Hayes frowned. 'No idea. Maybe it's something to do with the fertilizers put on the arable land round here – or perhaps it takes time for the birds to come back after the builders' disturbance. No dawn chorus to wake you up at least.'

Mason shook his head. 'No birds singing round here to be sure. Spooky, my Meg calls it.'

Hayes ushered him out, mentally noting a few more queries to put to the forensic team. He wandered out to the back garden gate and took a view of the house from the public footpath across the field. The conservatory glowed in the grey atmosphere, the orchid blooms seeming to float like exotic fish in a spotlit aquarium.

He decided to shoot back to the station. After a few words with Frame, he left the house, with the disturbing impression that any clues to the killer's identity were dissolving in the mist of soft rain slowly obscuring the false tropical oasis of Sandy Prentice's orchid house.

The Superintendent's PA pounced on him as soon as he entered the station, marching him to the big guy's office like an absconder.

Supt Waller was a bull of a man, fiftyish and full of guile, an experienced officer immured in traditional methods and none too enthusiastic about detectives of Hayes' calibre who he guessed were using his patch as a stepping stone to pastures greener than Renham.

'Well, nice of you to drop in, Hayes,' he said acidly, glowering at the untidy pile of papers on his desk. 'Bloody awful mess, this. Woman left dead in her own house for days on end and no one so much as takes a passing interest.' He stabbed at the pathologist's report, eyeing Hayes with rancour. 'All right, sit down. And let's shed some light on this scientific twaddle. Maggots, it says. Bloody hell. What a way to pin down time of death! Fill me in, Hayes. What progress have you made?'

'Nothing specific – we're still trying to establish her movements. Sandy Prentice was an incomer like all the others in Didcot Drive. They're not country folk, not in each other's pockets like the villagers. Nobody missed her and the only decent witnesses are a retired couple living next door and the cleaner, a kid called Melanie Crabbe who the local bobby knows through complaints from her neighbours. I thought I might check up on the boyfriend there, see what he's been up to: he might have got the impression from Melanie that the place was worth going over and it all got a bit out of hand. She was stabbed, of course, not unheard of when robberies go wrong.'

'Found the weapon?'

'Not yet, but—' Hayes hastened to smooth over the paucity of his progress and moved on to elaborate on the professor's findings detailed in the lab reports littering the Superintendent's desk. At the end of a hurried résumé, the big man irritably swept the papers into a file.

'Now what about formal identification? No next-of-kin, I see.'

'Next item on my list, sir. I was just about to arrange a meeting with Prentice's solicitor and see if he—'

'Hardcastle.'

Hayes stopped short as the Super swooped through his agenda like a samurai sword.

'Now listen to me, Chief Inspector. I've already had Hardcastle on to me about your arrogant behaviour: telling the sergeant to make him stand in line for an appointment like a bloody magistrate's clerk. Understand this, Hayes. Hardcastle runs a big operation in this town and has the ear of the top brass in Oxford, so giving Hardcastle a casual put-off's not going to win you any medals with the people who matter, and when a lawyer complains to me about one of my officers I don't feel too happy myself. You've made absolutely no progress in this case as far as I can see and it's the first few days of any investigation that are likely to be of any use at all, as well you know. What am I to say to the press? You can't keep a case like this under cover. Women all over the country, women living alone, are terrified this sort of thing can happen to them and the police take ten days to find out about it.'

'Yes, sir, but if I may say so the delay in discovering the body is a considerable handicap to our enquiries. Sod's law the next door neighbours were on holiday. Witnesses are bad enough if you catch them on the spot, but with hindsight information gets hazy and the victim was, like her neighbours, a newcomer, a comparatively recent arrival in Newton Greys who seemed to have made little impression on the local scene and worked freelance, apparently moving about from job to job both in London and Oxford.'

The Superintendent seemed unimpressed by Hayes' outburst, and was about to launch into a counterblast as the phone rang. He picked it up, waving dismissively as Hayes rose to go. As he reached the door, Waller covered the mouthpiece and fired his parting shot.

'Wait! Don't forget what I said about Hardcastle, Hayes. You make an appointment and get yourself over to his office in double quick time. And before you put your feet up any more on this inquiry, I want to see a formal identification on my desk. Pronto.'

Roger Hayes closed the door and recognized depression like a black dog at his heels. The old fart was right: he was getting nowhere with this case.

Twelve

He glanced at his watch: six fifteen, and a distinct mellowing of the atmosphere in the building as darkness fell. It was too late to phone Hardcastle, which was a bit of luck as Hayes felt ill-prepared for a run-in with a stroppy lawyer. Similarly, Prentice's accountant was on his hit list but he had barely scratched the surface of the dead woman's papers. The puzzle of her ample income might well be solved by a bequest from an aunt, as Mrs Mason had said, but maybe not . . .

He got some coffee from the machine and trailed back to his office to rake through the house-to-house reports his sergeant had laid prominently on the desk. After a desultory assessment of the lack of insight from any of Sandy Prentice's neighbours, he leaned back in his chair and mulled over the progress so far. It didn't take long. A new angle was called for, a professional's view of the bloody woman's activities and the means by which she maintained a lifestyle that included the cash purchase of a very expensive car and a wardrobe indicating a social round well beyond the range of a peripatetic hairdresser.

He shuffled through his notes and jotted down the address of the accountant's firm in north Oxford together with the address of the car dealership that had supplied the MG. Bugger Hardcastle: he'd tackle the accountant first thing in the morning and leave the solicitor for afters.

He brightened. Making a plan of even the flimsiest sort

cleared the air, and with a sudden realization that his guts were gnawing away like a ferret he stuffed the notes in his briefcase, turned off the lights and shot out of the station with all the semblance of a strong tailwind howling behind him.

Hayes drew up outside the house in Didcot Drive and nodded to the constable on the gate. A WPC and Sergeant Buller were relaxing at the kitchen table with mugs of coffee, the space between them strewn with garage bills and petrol receipts with which Buller was presumably trying to gauge information about the victim's movements. They scrambled to their feet as the Chief Inspector breezed in, and after a brief exchange about the car in the garage Hayes hurried into the telly room to extract all the files concerned with her financial outgoings.

Spending the next hour trawling through the woman's surprisingly detailed accounts and cross-referencing with bank statements left him with the clear impression that Sandy Prentice was no fool. Even so, the hairdressing payments hardly balanced the hefty outgoings and a considerable volume of cash passed seamlessly into her current account at irregular intervals. The tax returns passed before his glazed eyes like indecipherable hieroglyphics.

He packed up all the relevant papers and realized that the stomach rumblings were now off the Richter scale. Waving cheerfully at the duo in the kitchen, he drove off at speed in search of a gastronomic blow-out at a pub in Thame that specialized in mixed grills for heroes.

The place was dark and smoky, the ceiling pickled saffron by nicotine fumes, the saloon bar packed. He elbowed his way to the bar and downed a pint of lager like a castaway on a desert island. The barman greeted the spiky haired bloke with the *faux* bonhomie that goes with the job and is especially robust for police officers above the rank of sergeant. Hayes was very familiar with this particular hostelry, which lay equidistant from his old stamping ground and his new placement in Renham. He was not particularly keen on pubs, especially those redesigned with mock-Victorian knick-knacks and mock-Michelin-starred food. But the Lamb & Flag was OK and the publican friendly, a chancy business when a policeman in the bar made drinkers edgy.

Hayes laughed politely at the barmaid's joke about a recently carpeted gay police commissioner and moved into the back room, where tables set out with paper cloths and tin ashtrays made no appeal to lovers with a candlelit supper *à deux* in mind.

The snug was dimly lit and the few tables occupied by well-satisfied diners already into their coffees and brandies. The waitress grinned and pushed him to a table near the toilets, the only one free. But as he relaxed into his seat, a girl rose from a group on the far side of the room and wriggled between the diners towards the cloakroom. Hayes paused, eyeing the slim figure with a mixture of surprise and irritation. It was the new detective constable, Robbins, and he was in no mood for any chit-chat about the darned Prentice case.

She sighted him with a tinge of embarrassment and paused hesitantly as he half rose. Then she smiled and stepped across.

'Whoops! Didn't mean to disturb you – you must be starving like us. We've been at it all evening.' She lifted a hand and indicated the rest of her party, clearly a late booking like himself and still in the process of arguing over the menu. 'We've been hanging about for our friend Delphi to finish her rehearsal – she's been booked as accompanist to Florian Brandt and Johnny's been helping her with the programme.'

Hayes whistled. 'The German tenor?' He eyed the two girls on Robbins's table, each deeply into the pros and cons of the dish of the day, the voice of the single man with them rising with playful irritation at their fierce debate.

'Yes.' Jenny Robbins shot a challenging glance. 'Won't you join us? Johnny could do with some male support. You're keen on music yourself, I heard. I promise not to mention the investigation.'

She stood her ground, her auburn hair tied back in a ponytail, the fullness of her breasts outlined in a white T-shirt. He was tempted.

'Actually, I've bought a ticket for his recital. Chances are the Prentice job might still be hanging on but Brandt's a magical performer. I live in hope.'

'My friend Pippa over there – the one with the dark curly hair – is PA to the festival director. Come over. Give me a couple of minutes and I'll introduce you.'

She disappeared into the Ladies and Hayes decided to chance it. Partying with fellow-officers was usually a no-no in his book, especially junior officers with sex appeal, a situation which might boomerang on a man still tiptoeing round a new job and inevitably a subject of speculation in the canteen.

He called the waitress. 'Mary. OK if I move? Some friends of mine are sitting over there.'

She shot a glance at the lively trio at the far table. 'Johnny Todd's a mate of yours?' she said, then added with a giggle, 'Never would have guessed you needed a piano tuner.'

Hayes stiffened. 'Didn't know myself till five minutes ago.'

Thirteen

Jenny Robbins relaxed with a glass of Chardonnay and regarded the rest of the party with bemusement. She was the outsider here and no mistake. The talk over dinner had ranged from a dispute about Brandt's interpretation of the Fauré 'Serenade' to his choice in waistcoats. She felt distinctly odd man out in this little group, while Hayes, after an initial hesitation, joined their esoteric banter with enthusiasm.

The star of the evening was clearly Delphi, introduced to Hayes as Delphine Chambers, another resident of Newton Greys and a girl whose career since leaving the Royal College had floundered between stints as an accompanist and infrequent bookings at minor music festivals. Roger Hayes felt a stab of empathy, the poor girl's career on the concert circuit obviously making no waves. He watched her expressive gestures with fascination, coming to the conclusion that the piano tuner, Johnny Todd, was clearly besotted.

'What's the programme, apart from the Fauré?'

'Chausson.' Delphi turned to Hayes, focusing on their new companion for the first time. 'Some Schubert, and Hahn's "Venezia" as a finale. The Oxford recital's a run-in for Wigmore Hall.' She frowned, her brows set in an elfin face, the impression of impishness enhanced by a boyish haircut exposing small ears set close to her head, only one lobe pierced to accommodate a diamond stud which flashed with all the authenticity of many very expensive carats. She wore a ruby mohair sweater, her ringless hands fluttering constantly as she spoke.

'The finale is the problem,' Johnny Todd broke in. 'We've been trying to line it up with a recording of Brandt's but he doesn't get here till Friday and Delphi needs to soften the tone.'

'You have accompanied him before though, haven't you?'

'You can say that again.'

'Don't worry about it,' Johnny reassured her, 'his bark's worse than his bite. I'll back you up. Don't fight it, Delphi, or it'll all end in tears.'

He grabbed her hands, cradling the nervous fingers under his own ham-like fists. Hayes finished his coffee and rose.

'I've got some work to do before I turn in. I'll say good-night.' He smiled. 'Thanks for inviting me over – perhaps we could do this again sometime?'

Delphi grinned. 'If you're going to be there on the night, as they say, why don't you join us afterwards? Pippa's organized a little "soirée",' she said wryly, wrinkling her nose, 'for the maestro. You don't happen to speak German, do you? He'd love that.'

''Fraid not. But I'd be delighted to accept – if I'm free by then,' he added with a glance at Jenny Robbins.

'Actually we're off too – I'm taking Delphi home,' Johnny said, patting her knee, 'but the other girls are getting a taxi. My van doesn't run to back seats.'

'Can I give you a lift?' offered Hayes.

The dark haired girl flashed a smile, her eyes sparkling with mischief.

'Great! Jenny and I share a house in Newton Greys, so it's one stop.' Pippa eyed Jenny's boss with frank approval. Distinctly dishy and certainly no flanneller when it came to music talk.

'Right then. My car's outside when you're ready.' He

strode off to the bar to pay his bill, leaving the rest to shrug into coats and kiss all round. Hayes was buoyant: getting a break like that had cleared his head, and now even the prospect of a further three rounds sparring with the Prentice accounts no longer seemed unsustainable.

They strolled to Hayes' car, waving their farewells to Delphi and the piano tuner as they departed in a swirl of gravel from the pub car park. Hayes set off with the girls, the mood distinctly edgy. Pippa's voice was low, almost confiding, as she leaned forward from the back seat.

'No prizes for guessing Delphi's worried sick about this bloody concert, Roger. Hope she can cool it before Brandt shows up. He can be very prima donna even for a minor star on the festival programme, which is saying something, German tenors with little sex appeal being, as a rule, a minority interest.'

'Terrific tonal quality though,' put in Hayes, 'and the recording company are giving his tour loads of publicity, even a couple of feature articles in the weekend papers.' Hayes glanced in the rear-view mirror as the two shadowy faces danced spasmodically into view. 'I've got tickets for his Wigmore Hall recital too, as a matter of fact.'

'You're a real fan then?' Jenny Robbins said, a note of incredulity rising like a fish to bait.

'Well, sort of. More curiosity. I heard him at a concert in Amsterdam when I was on holiday a couple of years ago. Marvellous voice. I wondered if the acoustics were playing to his advantage but the London crowd are very discriminating and it's pretty well a box office sell out.'

'Enough of all this music talk!' Jenny cut in. 'How about some nice gossip? You fancied Delphi, didn't you, guv?' Her tone was teasing and Hayes' happy mood took a dive. His professional standing with any WPC was a touchy issue; maybe fraternizing, even as Brandt fans, had been a mistake.

'Jenny, stop bitching about Delphi,' Pippa snapped, her voice rising as she pressed forward, placing a hand on Hayes' shoulder. 'Delphi's had a row with her parents – and I asked her to share the house with us for a bit. Time she cut the apron strings and got out of her parents' place. She's twenty-six, for God's sake.'

'Perhaps she's too skint to go it alone. Does she intend to move to London?'

'Eventually. But the gigs are few and far between and being an accompanist wasn't first choice.'

'It never is. Playing second fiddle's hard graft.'

'Delphi could well afford to rent somewhere in Oxford.' Jenny sounded almost petulant.

'I suspect she doesn't want to get too cosy with Johnny. It's a funny relationship. He was the guy who got her a top agent. In his job he gets to know all the big noises on the music scene.'

'Anyway, what about her piano?' Jenny persisted. 'There's no room at the cottage for a bloody concert grand.'

'Her father's put his foot down. Thought by refusing her permission to take the Bechstein she'd back off. But Johnny's moving her old upright from her studio upstairs – he's trying to book a bloke to help. I said she could have the dining room till she made other plans.'

'Well, thanks a million, Pippa. You could have asked me!'

'Yeah, sorry. It was a spur of the moment thing. I felt sorry for her. Her mother's a cow, she already keeps Maurice tied to the house and winds up Mr Chambers to lean on Delphi. She's a spoiled brat, I give you that, but being faced with earning a living instead of living off Daddy's money might do her a bit of good.'

'Nothing to do with keeping her cool before the festival by any chance?'

Hayes half listened to their bickering in the back seat,

assuming the house belonged to the Cooper girl, Robbins as a lodger having to fit in with any shift in the arrangement. They seemed to have forgotten all about their driver during this girly squabble, their voices rising in irritation.

It was only when he drew up in Church Lane and asked, 'Which house?' that they broke off their tit-for-tat, Robbins subsided into embarrassment and Pippa chimed in with, 'Next along. Holly Cottage. The one with the broken gate. Hey, thanks, Roger. Sorry about our little spat. Won't you come in for a coffee?'

'No, but thanks again. Nice evening, nice friends, nice talk.'

They scrambled out, their faces outlined in the bright moonlight, the lane unlit.

He drove off, grinning like a gargoyle, congratulating himself on no longer having to share his own pad. All three girls were interesting, though on reflection Delphine Chambers would be a handful. But undeniably beautiful and a pianist among the starry firmament compared with the amateurish tinkling of the ill-fated Sandy Prentice.

Funny, though, that piano tuner being a link between them . . .

Fourteen

Hayes arrived late next morning, only logging on at the police station after ten. He had taken a detour to Newton Greys, parked at the rear of the pub and spent the next hour pacing out the locality of the murder. The air was clear, the autumn golds already fading to dull greens and copper. He tramped from the pub to the church, noting the village hall and post office and passing the cottage where he had dropped off the girls the previous evening.

It had been a good night out, and a strange coincidence meeting the piano tuner informally like that. He remembered Sandy Prentice's cleaner insisting that he often called at the house. Wouldn't the test of a good tuner be the infrequency of his visits? Constant tinkering with Sandy's 'joanna' hinted at a more intimate than professional friendship.

He jogged across the field from the upper end of the village via the public footpath which brought him to Didcot Drive, Sandy's house and the Masons' each having a small gate in the hedge giving access to the back gardens. Hayes timed his route and calculated the get-away of any intruder either to the highway or back to the pub car park where a vehicle could stand unnoticed all day. The Bell, catering largely to locals, still opened its doors in the evening at five thirty and, according to PC Frame, enjoyed a loyal clientele attracted by Mollie, the publican's wife, plus a friendly welcome. He decided to sample the Bell himself at sixish – see what kind of regulars were drawn to a pint on their way home from work.

He was packing up the Prentice papers ready for his appointment with the accountant at eleven thirty when his sergeant knocked at the door.

Bellamy was a steady worker, familiar with the goings-on in an area encompassing agricultural holdings and small industrial units, a blossoming conurbation fed by the increasing population of Oxford and its satellite towns. The efficient road links had enhanced the attractions of Renham, and new housing developments were already threatening to dilute its small market-town appeal.

'Yes, Bellamy? Any progress?'

'One interesting turn-up, sir. A couple of drunks got into a fight outside the Bell in Newton Greys last night. The publican called us in and the pair of them spent the night in the cells – released after the Super was persuaded to intervene.'

'No charges?'

'None. One of these characters is something of a local celebrity – if bad lads count that is. Maurice Chambers. His dad got on to our top brass and must have waved a magic wand because his son's far from popular in the village and,' his voice dropped to whisper, 'has form.'

'Form?'

'Young Chambers killed a boy on a bike a few years back and left the poor little bugger in the road. Hit and run, in other words. A van driver chased him and Chambers was convicted of everything the court could throw at him. He spent two and a half years inside.'

Hayes jolted to attention. 'Chambers? Any relation to a girl called Daphne – er no, Delphi? That's it.'

Bellamy nodded, impressed by the new boss's swift grasp of the local scene.

'His father owns two car showrooms, one in Thame and

the other in Aylesbury – real gold mines, though rumour has it the wife runs the business. I had a word with Frame first thing and he filled me in. The family live at the Old Rectory and Mrs Chambers 'as got her finger in all the local stuff, chairman of the Newton Greys Village Hall Committee, church warden, you name it, Frame says.'

'And this lady does all this in her spare time – after running two garage outlets, you say?'

'Started up as Chambers' secretary over twenty years ago, so I'm told. Chambers' garages hold the franchises for Audi and Volkswagen, not what you'd call small beer, eh, sir?'

'And the other man?'

'A fireman called Gerry Long. Decent type, not your usual pub brawler but bears a grudge against Chambers. Uncle of the dead boy. Chambers 'as got a nerve going into the village pub at all, if you ask me. But with no vehicle licence it's a long walk to the Red Lion in Shelton and he can't ride a bike because of his knee. His mum's got her work cut out with that one. She tries to keep him off the sauce and tells everyone he's working on her sales team but it's hard to believe. According to Gary Frame, Maurice Chambers 'as never had a proper job in ten years. Been dried out since his release so the family says but she can't keep him out of the pub for ever and he's been seen after dark pushing empties in the recycling bin more than once a week.'

'How old's this fellow?'

'Must be in his mid-thirties. Do you want a report?'

'Some notes from the arresting officer would be useful. Funnily enough, I met his sister last night – she's accompanying a German singer who's one of the big names booked for the music festival in Oxford.'

Bellamy looked blank, his own preference veering more towards golden oldies, the guys with real talent like Nat King Cole.

Hayes glanced at his watch. 'Christ! Is that the time? I'm

off. If the Super asks, I'm on my way to check out some legal points with the Prentice advisers. Don't get too specific but if anything new turns up get me on my mobile. Oh, and make a run into London with Buller and see what you can find out about the purchase of Prentice's MG. I can't find any big cash withdrawal in her bank statement to match up with the payout to the dealer.'

He started packing up his papers and Bellamy turned to go. But as he reached the door, Hayes called him back.

'What's wrong with Chambers' knee?'

'Got smashed up when his BMW hit a tree in the car chase after the hit-and-run. Left him with a stiff leg. Long is reported as saying it was a pity it wasn't his neck what got broke.'

'Bitter words.'

'Yeah. Plenty of people reckon he got off light after killing that boy and leaving him in the road.'

Hayes nodded, mulling over Bellamy's gossip all the way to Oxford.

The accountant was far from a star witness, his understanding of the dead woman's cash flow being infuriatingly vague.

'What about tax returns?'

The man was on the verge of retirement at a guess, and to Hayes' mind could hardly wait for the golden handshake and a permanent date with his golf clubs.

'You must agree, Mr Fuller,' Hayes persisted, 'the income is fluid.'

'The nursing homes and clinics paid retainers, of course, and detailed invoices were submitted. My secretary will give you a list of the establishments if you wish. All perfectly in order, I assure you, Chief Inspector.'

'But all this cash washing around, indicated by her paying in book here,' he said, stabbing at the sheets of bank statements and receipts pushed under the man's nose. 'Hardly tips,' he added coldly.

Thomas Fuller had been an accountant to university Fellows, councillors, a surgeon or two . . . all decent, God-fearing folk. Mrs Prentice had been a charming client who presented her annual returns in excellent order. He drew himself up. Enough was enough.

'I don't know what you are implying, Inspector Hayes, but all my people are highly respectable. This appalling attack on Mrs Prentice was obviously an aggravated burglary. It could happen to anyone. The lady had no dishonest dealings of any kind, and I will go to my grave in the sure belief that the poor lady is yet another victim of these violent times.'

Hayes sighed. He was wasting his time. Mr bloody Fuller knew even less than he about the deceased and had clearly been enchanted by a woman with just the sort of glamour to attract an old buffer like that.

He rose, reclaiming his documents and holding out a hand which Fuller reluctantly shook in an approximation of business cordiality. He muttered a brief instruction into the intercom and on his way out the girl handed Hayes a typewritten list, which he thrust into his briefcase with a curt nod before hurrying back to the car.

In no mood for yet more professional denials, Hayes nevertheless determined to make a day of it and telephoned the solicitor's office to insist on an immediate appointment. 'I am investigating a brutal murder and have no leisure to fit in with Mr Hardcastle's diary,' he bellowed at the unfortunate secretary.

'Mr Hardcastle is with clients in Birmingham. All day,' she added with relish.

'Well, get on to him and say it's important.'

She left him hanging on, his impatience souring his empty belly like a bad bout of dyspepsia.

'Mr Hardcastle has kindly agreed to forgo his lunch

appointment tomorrow to accommodate you, Chief Inspector,' she said with asperity. 'You may use one of the partners' parking spaces at the rear and he will expect you at one.'

She cut him off with the finality of a bacon slicer and Hayes sighed. But you'd have to hand it to the woman for sheer style, he admitted.

As it happened, barging into the middle of Hardcastle's lunch hour was the first break in an investigation assuming the complexity of a maze whose alleys led only to the mystery of the incomprehensible allure of a woman who now lay in a mortuary cabinet.

Fifteen

The station was curiously quiet all afternoon; Buller and Bellamy in London pinning down the details of the victim's purchase of the second-hand MG, the rest of the team trawling through the village for personal titbits about the woman's movements.

As he was going through the forensic report yet again the difficulties attending the investigation of a death which had occurred twelve days prior to the discovery of the body stuck in his craw like a fishbone, the irritation following his fruitless interview with the accountant now distilled to bleak despair.

Jenny Robbins knocked tentatively at the half-open door.

He looked up. 'Yes?'

'I thought you'd want to know how we got on with sifting through the village recycling bin. We all but put everything through a colander,' she said, the lift of her eyebrow speaking volumes.

'Lucky old you. Any joy?'

'We found the empty Bollinger bottle – it's gone for fingerprint tests.'

'Intact?'

'Absolutely. Did you think it might have been the murder weapon?'

'A possibility. Smashed in temper, the neck of a broken bottle thrust at the woman, perhaps in the course of a fight.'

She looked dubious. 'A jealous boyfriend? Sandy Prentice seems to have been a likeable sort, we haven't found anyone to say a bad word about her.'

'You never met her yourself? At church? She seems to have been on decent terms with the vicar, helped out at his summer concert I gather.'

'She didn't go to church. I saw her around, in the post office a couple of times, but not to speak to. She didn't really spend a lot of time in the village. Have you spoken to the vicar?'

'Not yet. I'm still trying to construct some sort of profile. The woman's professional life might be instructive. Oh, here,' he said, scrabbling through his briefcase. 'Take this. It's a list of the nursing homes and clinics she worked for. The accountant said Prentice received retainers on a regular basis but was paid individually by each client, in cash presumably, not much in the way of small cheques passing through her paying in book. I want you and Sergeant Bellamy to visit all of them and see what you can find out. Get a note of her regulars over the past six months, tap the nurses for any gossip – you know the form. If anything strikes you as unusual I'll run over there myself. These chi-chi detox clinics are stuffed with rich addicts, she may have put the squeeze on someone. Sandy Prentice didn't run up a bank balance like hers just from chatting up the punters.'

'OK. Funny thing is, women confide stuff to their hairdresser they'd never share with a best friend. The juicy items I've heard waiting for a blow-dry would make you blink. A hairdresser is like a psychiatrist, a sympathetic ear, someone who's not family or even – to hear some of them rabbit on – people who have any real identity at all. Faceless. It's a sort of therapy to some women. But murder? What sort of person would kill her like that?'

'Someone with no other course of action open to them.'

'Blackmail? She cut men's hair too, you know. Would be easy to strike up a relationship with a vulnerable guy under treatment who, when he gets out into the real world, finds his temporary lover dangerously demanding.'

Hayes frowned, blown along by the girl's enthusiasm, wondering if it was wise to share his private anxieties about the case with this red-headed constable with promotion on her mind.

She was still speaking, her voice low and insistent '. . . and if it's true she was killed by someone driven to drastic measures that's more likely to be unpremeditated, isn't it? An act of passion. You said the killer could be someone with no other course of action. But if he went to her house to settle up with her and the row got out of hand, what about a weapon? If we're looking for someone who killed her in a fit of rage, he wouldn't arm himself first.'

'Something to hand?'

'You're still hooked up on the broken bottle idea, aren't you, sir? But the SOCO boys found not so much as a fragment of broken glass, apart from the wine goblet Tansy accidentally smashed when she found the body.'

'Forget it. The missing champagne bottle bugged me, that's all. How did it get in the recycling bin? Sandy Prentice wouldn't have put it there – her dustbin had a couple of empty bottles and she's not the sort of person to my mind who would bother with environmental considerations. Here, take this away.'

He thrust the list at her in a dismissive gesture but she stood her ground, her mouth tightening with determination.

'If the killer struck her with whatever came to hand there's something that bugs me too, sir. We've searched high and low and nowhere, not even in her car, could we find her scissors. Crimpers guard their scissors like crazy – won't lend them to anyone else, keep them to hand like we would attach ourselves to a watch or a ring. How about if

Sandy invited some guy over ostensibly for a trim and he tried to break off a relationship – or even pay her off, if your blackmail theory's correct? They get into a fight. She goes for him with her scissors. He grabs them from her and defensively stabs her a couple of times. She bleeds like a stuck pig. He loses his head when she starts screaming for help, terrified of being reported to the police and had up in court. He stabs her in the throat to make her shut up and when she passes out he legs it back to his car, leaving her to die.'

Hayes gave a slow hand-clap, eyeing her flushed cheeks with amusement.

'Great scenario, Robbins. You should give up this police lark and write for the TV soaps.'

She grabbed the list he pushed over to her and stalked out, slamming the door.

Hayes leaned back, still smiling, relishing the hot-tempered response of Constable Robbins. Mind you, he conceded, the girl had a point. The description of the wounds in the pathologist's report might well tie in with a pair of razor sharp scissors, and the fact remained the bloody things *were* missing.

The knock on the door was insistent, breaking off his line of thought. Without waiting for a reply Bellamy stepped in, his expression eager as a cocker spaniel's.

'Excuse me, sir. Me and Buller just got back.'

'From the car showroom?'

'Yes, sir. You'll never believe this. The Prentice woman arrived to check over the MG with a boyfriend.'

'Name?'

'No name but a pretty good description. The sales manager was impressed. The boyfriend knew his stuff, went over the engine like a pro, checked every nut and bolt, he says.'

'So what? Buying a second-hand car with her hard-earned

cash, the woman would be out of her mind not to get some expert advice.'

'Yeah, sure, that's what we thought. But this guy handed over the cash from his own wallet. Wads of it. No wonder the salesman was impressed.'

'Whose name on the receipt?'

'Hers. He said it was a birthday present for the lady and she looked cock-a-hoop over it, practically licked the bloke all over, and no wonder.'

'You said you got a description.'

'You bet we did. The secretary in the office confirmed it – wished she had a boyfriend with a wad of fifties in his back pocket, I shouldn't wonder. Over a year ago now but they was both sure of the details. Not too many customers like that. Young chap, they said, longish hair, none too matey with the garage people but all over the Prentice woman. Had a bit of a limp: nothing too noticeable – no stick nor nothin' – but both witnesses agreed he was a bit hoppy.'

'You got signed statements?'

'The kid in the office typed them out on the spot. Not exactly a big break, sir, is it? We never really thought she could afford to buy a car like that herself, did we?'

'He could have just been a bagman, keeping her money in his wallet to turn the attention off her. She wouldn't want a used car salesman to get the idea she was walking about with bundles of notes stuffed up her knickers, would she?'

Bellamy looked crestfallen but obstinately stuck in there. 'Yeah, right, sir. But still, whoever the boyfriend was we know there's some bloke out there she trusted enough to put on a show like that, if that was how she wanted to play it, don't we?'

Sixteen

The Bell was Roger Hayes' idea of an old-fashioned country pub. It wasn't, of course. The brasswork was a bit too shiny and the mock-leather banquettes were a bit too slippery, but the low lighting softened the effect and no 'mood music' drowned the buzz of small talk which lowered perceptibly as the now familiar detective inspector breezed in.

The place was half full, the regulars already hogging most of the high stools at the bar, the rest of the Happy Hour drinkers comprising men in office suits, a smattering of farm labourers crowding round the fruit machine and two young women in deep conversation in the far corner. The barmaid greeted him warmly, her dangling earrings all a-go-go as her nervous glance swept the length of the bar.

'Half a pint of Carlsberg, love,' he said, lighting a cigarette before settling at a corner table. The landlord sidled in from the back, pushing a heavy-metal type ahead of him and shouting, 'Gina, ducky, pour a pint for my friend Jason here – on the house.'

The lad looked pretty chuffed and started off to join the boys at the machine. Hayes caught his sleeve and smiled, inviting him in that special CID tone: 'Here, join me, Jason, I'd like some company.' The lad's confidence fled and he slid into a seat at Hayes' table, accepting a cigarette with an anxious nod. He sipped his beer, eyeing Hayes from under lowered brows. Jason Pickett was a stocky character, the heavy build bulked out in a black leather jacket, ragged jeans spilling over biker's boots.

'Yeah?'

Hayes moved in close, his voice barely a whisper.

'I've been wanting a quiet word with you, Jason. As a local you can fill me in on a few details. I might even be able to shake a few quid from the petty cash box if you play the game. OK?'

Jason drew on his cigarette, saying nothing, his leathers giving off a whiff of motor oil and sweat.

'How about this fight in the car park here last night? You were here?'

He nodded. 'I fetch Mel on me bike when she's finished up in the kitchen at closing time. She don't like walking home on her tod since the murder.'

'Thought you might. Well, the two of them are off the hook – escaped with a caution – but what I have to know is, what was the fight about? Pissed out of their minds, but still . . .'

'Chambers was rat-arsed as usual but the fireman was stone cold sober. He come in late, just before last orders. He don't live round here and barged in as if he was looking for trouble. He clocked Chambers up at the bar and the place went dead quiet. It was his nephew what died and—'

'In the hit-and-run?'

'Yeah. Poor little sod. Only nine years old, on his way home from his gran's, they said.'

'But Chambers served his time, didn't he? And it was a few years ago now, wasn't it? Why the aggro?'

'It wasn't just that. Morry Chambers lost his licence, see, and the other bloke, I forget 'is name, swore he'd seen him driving a red car out Chatterdon way less than a month ago. They started rowing and Mollie told them to sling their 'ook. Morry just grinned and the fireman grabbed hold of him and fetched him a real wallop, sent Chambers crashing into the bar, knocking the stools over. He kicked Morry in the ribs as he lay on the floor, shouting he'd kill him himself if Chambers ever got behind a wheel again. Two of the regulars shoved them outside and Charlie called time but it blew up into a real headbanger in the car park and somebody called the police.'

'He couldn't be right about Chambers driving though, could he? Chambers is kept on a short rein by his mum, so I've heard, won't let him off the leash if she can help it.'

Jason's sly grin lit up his acne-pitted face. 'Sez you. Bloody Iris thinks she's got him taped but she'd need eyes in the back of her bleedin' head to keep that one in line.'

'Nobody took this story seriously, did they? The fireman's claim that he'd spotted Chambers driving a car in Chatterdon? It wasn't reported.'

Jason shrugged. 'Still rankles though, losing a little kid on the road like that. His mum went right off her 'ead for months after and is still on the tablets, Mel told me. And no wonder. Accidents happen but a hit-and-run, specially a fucking arsehole like Chambers, ain't never forgiven, not in this village. Not never.'

Hayes slipped a tenner under the table into Jason's oil-stained fist and took a long draught of lager. The lad frowned, pocketing the money with a hurried glance round the bar. Did the tenner make him a 'snout'? He shrugged, stubbing out his fag end with a crafty wink at his unexpected benefactor.

The pub was filling up, the air now thick with nicotine fumes mingling with the hint of smoky beefburgers wafting from the back kitchen. Jason raised a hand, shielding his mouth with a gesture worthy of a drama queen as he placed another morsel at Hayes' disposal.

'The Chambers lot ain't flavour of the month in this village – the old man's all right but the woman's a bossy cow, tries to put her oar in where it's not wanted and some folk round here are stupid enough to take their money and don't see what's round the corner. The squire and Lady Honora ain't like that – everyone respects them, see – but Iris bloody Chambers can't see it. They've lived here for four years or more, moved into the Old Rectory from a place in Thame, and she fancies herself as Queen Bee, but they could be here for a hundred years and it wouldn't be long enough. You can't buy respect and that fucking Morry Chambers gets up everyone's nose with his la-di-da talk and everythin'. Been inside, o' course, a three-year stretch reduced to a bit over two, and most people round here wouldn't hold it against him if it wasn't for leaving the kid to die in the road.'

'Bitter words, Jason. I met the sister the other night. She seemed decent enough.'

'Must take after her dad. Don't see much of her but I'll tell you somethin' I've not let slip before. Mel told me to shut up about it, she don't want me to get involved, see?'

Hayes said nothing, wondering if lobbing tenners at this new informer would only lead to a dribble of useless gossip he could get for free if he sat about in the Bell for a few nights.

'I seen Maurice Chambers on the path behind the Prentice place the day she died.'

'Which was?'

'Thursday the fourth of October,' he crowed.

'You remember the date exactly?'

'My birthday, weren't it? Mel told me the police had worked it out that Sandy croaked on my bleeding birthday. What about that! I'd took her grandad into Renham on the bus that morning to have his eyes tested. Silly old bugger won't go on my bike so we wasted money on bus fares. While we was on our way back we bumped into Mel's mum – market day, see, Mavis she always goes into Renham on Thursdays, does her shopping round the stalls. She grabs the old man and takes him off to the chip shop. Said she'd bring him back later after Ted got home with the van.'

'Not you?'

'Nah! Old Mavis wouldn't buy me two penn'orth a chips, not likely. By then I'd missed the twelve o'clock bus back and had bloody hours to hang about for the next one. We only get two each way to this dead-and-alive hole of a village so I spent me dinner hour playing pool with my mates. It was me bleedin' birthday, weren't it?' he added defensively.

'So?'

'Later, I had to leg it home from the crossroads. It was coming on to rain and I spotted this bloke on the footpath ahead of me. I was takin' the short cut across the fields and was feeling bloody hungry I can tell you. Taking old Jim into town had cost me best part of the day, give or take, and I'd missed me dinner an' all.'

Hayes finished his half-pint and buttoned his coat. 'Get on with it, man, I've not got all night.'

Jason leaned across the table, his stale breath causing Hayes to stiffen.

'It was Chambers all right,' he hissed. 'I'd know his gimpy walk a mile off.'

Roger frowned. 'Why pick on Chambers? It could have been anyone bundled up against the rain. Why didn't you come forward with this information if you were so sure?'

'I told you! Mel said, "Keep your trap shut, Jason. They'll twist what you say and before you know it the Chambers family'll have your guts for garters." They're a powerful influence in this place, believe me.'

'What time was this?'

'Comin' up for three, near enough.'

'Will you make a statement?'

Jason jumped up, jogging the table, upsetting his empty glass as he backed off.

'No way. I thought I was just giving you a tip, like. You're the fucking detective! You do the legwork. Mel was right, I should have kept buttoned up.'

He strode from the bar, leaving Hayes with a niggling suspicion that the villagers in Newton Greys were setting him up: getting their revenge on the poor bastard Chambers years after the unforgiven crime which had put him in prison and left him with no driving licence and a busted knee just so as he'd never forget.

Seventeen

Next morning Hayes decided the most urgent task was to get the body officially identified. With apparently no next-of-kin and no close friends in the village apart from the elderly Masons, it was a toss-up whether to wait and see if the solicitor would co-operate or whether to jump on another innocent bystander. He was juggling his options as Jenny Robbins knocked at the door.

'Excuse me, sir, I'm just off to Aylesbury with Sergeant Bellamy but I've typed a list of Sandy Prentice's telephone numbers you asked me to check.'

'Something cropped up?'

She grinned. A nice smile, he conceded, and no make-up to spoil the freckles speckling her nose. Hayes had never dated a redhead and found his thoughts drifting. He pulled himself up short and rose abruptly to replace a folder in the filing cabinet.

'Well, sir, the numbers you wanted identified were mostly colleagues' home numbers, apart from one woman who runs a private nursing agency plus a couple of London dress hire boutiques. The local numbers were for the church organist, a young chap called Terry Thurgood who runs the choir, an off-licence in Renham and mobile phone number for her cleaner's boyfriend, Jason Pickett. The oddity was the ex-directory number for the Old Rectory, the Chambers' house in the village. The number listed in the phone book rings in the housekeeper's room so presumably the private number on your list is for family use only.'

'Has the daughter, Delphi, moved in with you and Pippa?'

'Yesterday.' Her face darkened. 'It's not that I don't like the girl, but two's company if you see what I mean . . . The piano gets installed in the morning. Johnny Todd is seeing to it.'

'Any idea why she's fallen out with her family? The mother's the controlling type so I've heard.'

'Iris has her faults but Noel, that's Chambers Senior, is a bit of a layabout, leaves Iris to run the business, sees himself as a glorified non-executive director, and Maurice is literally a dead leg. I feel sorry for Iris: the men in her life are both charming but useless and Delphi's entirely wrapped up in her music, which leaves the mother to do everything. Delphi reckons the rows at home are worse than ever, Iris accusing Noel of all sorts of stuff and Maurice, who's the blue-eyed boy according to his sister, seems to play the parents off against each other.'

'The joys of family life. No wonder the girl's shipped out. Leave the list here, I'll work at it later. Oh, one more thing before you get back on the road: what's the local vicar like? Sensible chap?'

'You mean Harcourt? He's OK. Comes across a bit like a missionary who finds the natives still cannibals, but he means well. Copes with three parishes with only a lay-reader and a retired rural dean to help. But he's sensible enough when it comes to practical matters. Used to be an accountant before he got the Call.'

'I thought I might persuade him to identify the body. He knew Sandy Prentice well enough, didn't he?'

She looked doubtful. 'Well enough for a formal identification and not the sort to faint in the mortuary, if that's what you're worried about.'

He nodded, pushing her ahead of him into the hub of

activity in the Renham cop shop, where his team of eager and not so eager officers were being briefed by the Detective Superintendent.

Hayes managed to escape with an urgent plea of 'An appointment, sir. Mr Hardcastle. Mustn't keep him waiting,' and hurried to his car.

The meeting with Sandy Prentice's vicar went smoothly, the man taking the steps outside the mortuary with a positive spring in his step as Hayes ingratiated himself and led him inside. For himself he found the antiseptic smell of the place made him queasy, and their echoing footsteps as they were escorted to the viewing area all too much like a funeral march.

Hayes paused at the door, holding back his witness. 'You OK with this, Mr Harcourt?'

'No problem, Chief Inspector. Only too glad to help. Deathbed attendances are not a rarity in my calling, of course; it's tragic to discover how often an elderly person dies alone with no grieving relatives at the bedside. Young people too, it would seem from what one reads in the newspapers. Sadly, Mrs Prentice is not the first body to lie undiscovered, a telling indictment of "neighbourliness" in a village like ours.'

The identification went smooth as silk, and Hayes mentally gave Harcourt three cheers, peering at the ravaged features of the corpse not being something for the lily-livered. They parted in the car park, shaking hands with relief after an unpleasant job efficiently dealt with.

Hayes raced back to Renham just in time to make his appointment with the solicitor, whose offices occupied a grand house in the Market Square, its imposing façade graced with a brass plaque polished almost to illegibility. There were four partners, Hardcastle's name well placed after two senior partners whose reputations as local dignitaries registered even with Hayes. Clearly Hardcastle was a key member of an old-established firm which the Super was anxious not to offend.

Gerald Hardcastle greeted him at the door of his room, a disarming gesture which gave Hayes no small satisfaction augmented by the rich aroma of fresh coffee perking on a side table. A spotty youth in blazer and grey flannels placed a tray of sandwiches on the boss man's desk and sidled out, as well rehearsed as a royal page in a costume drama.

'On work experience,' Hardcastle whispered. 'We take two at a time, God knows why but it keeps the chairman of the Education Committee happy, a chum of our senior partner you know. They learn nothing, these boys, except how to make a decent cup of tea and fiddle the stamp money.'

Hardcastle was younger than Hayes had anticipated, forty or forty-five at the most, his hair thick and with just enough traces of silver to add that undeniable air of suavity. He wore the regulation striped suit and a blue shirt with what Hayes took to be a college tie, but the lapels were just that fraction wider than the normal business gear and as he bustled round the desk to pour coffee there was a flash of indigo silk lining, clearly the sort of tailoring only Savile Row could produce.

They small-talked their way through smoked salmon sandwiches and black coffee, Hardcastle returning his starched napkin to the tray as a discreet signal that 'Time is money'. They got down to business.

'Now, how can I help you, Chief Inspector?'

'Some details about the deceased, if you will. Information about her bequests, if Mrs Prentice made any that is.'

'Right.' Hardcastle cut to the bone, extracting names and dates almost too rapidly for Hayes to note down.

'Sandra Christine Prentice, age forty-two, divorced, no children. The value of her estate including house, contents and personal effects such as jewellery, car etc. in the region of a quarter of a million. In addition Mrs Prentice, as you may well know, had a healthy bank balance and various investments including shares in a local firm. There is an outstanding mortgage which is covered by insurance.'

'Recently acquired? The shareholding you mention. Since her move here?'

'Ah no. I handled the purchase of the house in Newton Greys and the shares were in her name some time before that. As a first-time buyer her capital was a consideration, of course, but as it happened she required only a small mortgage.'

'She inherited money from an aunt, I was informed.'

Gerald Hardcastle looked over his spectacles.

'Absolutely not. Where did you get that idea?'

Hayes shrugged. 'Local gossip. Why Newton Greys? Did she say?'

'No, Inspector. She mentioned an interest in the countryside, and her work involved travel in this area, of course. She attended patients in the formidably expensive Westlake Clinic plus an impressive list of nursing homes. Frankly, I thought the move unwise. I had meetings with the poor woman on several occasions and anticipated she was not the type to embrace rural pursuits or be content to live in the stultified atmosphere of a semi-rural cul-de-sac.'

His tone gave the impression that a small market town was not the location Gerald Hardcastle would willingly choose either, but he briskly moved on, his voice resuming the bland tones of legal prudence.

Hayes interrupted his seamless flow, impatient to cut to the chase. 'One thing. During the conveyancing work, you must have written to Mrs Prentice at her former address.'

'Quite so. Let me see.' He sifted through the file. 'Ah, yes. Flat 16, Porchester House, Paddington. I happen to know it, my cousin lives in the square. A very smart block of flats. Mrs Prentice and I chatted about the neighbourhood and she mentioned she shared the flat with a girlfriend but fancied having a house in the country all to herself. Hardly what I would call the real countryside, but near enough if you're coming from city streets I suppose.

'After the completion of the house purchase, I persuaded Mrs Prentice to make a will. At first she was reluctant. Clients are, I find, a little superstitious about wills, as if making sensible preparations for the disposal of one's goods is tempting Fate. She had no family to consider, but even so it tidies things up considerably if such matters are nicely in place.'

Hayes perked up. 'And who is the lucky beneficiary?'

The solicitor grinned. 'Apart from the Treasury – tax will claw a percentage from the estate, of course, and there will be other expenses including the funeral. Once the dust settles the person named in the Prentice will is a Mrs Marie O'Brien. I did my best to persuade my client to think again but she insisted the only person for whom she felt the need to provide was this former neighbour from her childhood in Battersea.' He allowed himself a discreet grimace.

'You disapproved?'

'Only because Mrs O'Brien is eighty-four years old. Hardly of an age likely to benefit although, as it turns out, the old lady may well live to be a hundred and a nice little nest egg to cushion her declining years cannot be unwelcome. I gather her benefactor paid the fees of a private nursing home in London, so, in retrospect, the choice was fortuitous.'

'Did she explain her relationship with Mrs O'Brien?'

'Nothing more than that she was kind to her in the past and a poor woman who deserved a comfortable retirement after years of struggle.'

'Obviously close . . . and Sandy Prentice must have been regularly in touch if she was financing this nursing home care. I shall have to talk to Mrs O'Brien – she may have information to assist with my enquiries. From the impression I get so far, Sandy Prentice would seem to have been a generous sort with not an enemy in the world. To die alone in a close-knit community and for her disappearance to remain unreported seems at odds with that.'

Hardcastle's response was hard to read, his curiosity about his client hedged about with professional neutrality. After a moment he decided to cross the line.

'As it happens I have met Mrs O'Brien. The old lady apparently shared my reservations about the will and insisted on making one herself. Mrs Prentice brought her along here to me and we hatched up a second will which seemed to put Mrs O'Brien's mind at rest. She is a down-to-earth person, in no way failing in mental capacities, her health good but for painful arthritis, which forced her to take up my client's offer to enter a nursing home. Mrs O'Brien named one of her foster-children who will, of course, benefit from a windfall which would never, except for the unexpected death of Mrs Prentice, have come his way, assuming as one would that the old lady would naturally predecease my client.'

'This O'Brien person was not comfortably off herself?'

'Indeed not! She had nothing except a state pension and, as I say, my client later bankrolled the old lady's retirement through her own earnings. I would hazard a guess that Mrs Prentice came from an impoverished childhood and if Mrs O'Brien had been a neighbour, the old lady's former address would indicate no great riches there.'

He jotted down two addresses from his file and passed them over.

'At the time Mrs O'Brien called here to sign the will a year ago she rented a council house. Shortly after that she moved into the Gables, a retirement home in south London. Hardly a geriatric Cinderella story but a fairy godmother like Mrs Prentice is a rarity these days.'

'What happened to the husband?'

'They divorced ten years ago. Geoffrey Prentice then moved to Australia, remarried, and later died after an encounter with a shark. Not a lucky man. He was an engineer, worked in the car industry. Perhaps her ex-husband was the one to recommend she bought shares in Chambers' garages.'

Hayes bolted upright. 'Chambers' Autos? The place in Thame?'

Hardcastle nodded. 'A flourishing outlet, and there's another branch in the area, can't remember where exactly, but very efficiently run by Mrs Chambers it would seem. The firm was inherited by Noel and, strictly between ourselves, Inspector, having bumped into the man at the golf club on just about every occasion I've found time to make eighteen holes with my junior partner here, one would assume that Chambers himself is less interested in selling motor cars than was wise.'

They hurried through the finer details and Hayes rose to go, his mental picture of the dead woman even more confused.

Back in the car he called his sergeant. 'Still on the road, Bellamy?'

'Just on our way back, sir. Robbins and I've been to that Aylesbury clinic you asked us to check out. She walked round the grounds chatting up some of the patients while I worked the administrator's office. Guess what? Robbins got talking to some kid on detox who had a thing going with Maurice Chambers. It seems he got shoved in this Westlake Clinic by his mum as soon as he got released. Must have picked up some nasty habits while he was in clink.'

'When you get back to the station, get one of the lads to make out a full report on Maurice Chambers, will you? I got a tip that he was seen in the vicinity of the murder on the afternoon in question. I also want the fingerprint team to try and find an identifiable print on that champagne bottle retrieved from the recycling bin – with luck it might tie in this Chambers bloke, who has a few questions to answer. If you can get some facts for me to chase up I'll call in at the Old Rectory in the morning. You'd better come along, Bellamy. Pick me up from Haddenham at nine.'

Eighteen

Saturday morning dawned cold and clear, with no wind to strip the remaining yellow leaves from the avenue of poplars leading to the Old Rectory. Under direction Bellamy drove slowly, Hayes taking in the landscaping which had, at a guess, elevated a modest vicarage to the country house the Chambers aspired to. The building was early Victorian, an elegant metal canopy shielding the south side from the sun, the paintwork gleaming from recent maintenance. The house, no longer the unheated residence of a series of none too affluent clerics, had come into its inheritance at last, the new owners sparing no expense in renovation.

They stopped behind a high-sided van parked in front of the porch, surprised to find the main door wide open on this chilly October morning. Hayes rang the bell but no one came despite loud voices issuing from the landing, where a row was in full throttle. He stepped inside just as a girl's head appeared over the gallery rail circling the first floor and overlooking the oval hallway.

'Hey, Roger! Great. We could do with another strongman. Come up.'

It was Delphine Chambers, looking considerably more chirpy than on their previous meeting. His sergeant shot him a puzzled glance, unsure where this new inspector picked up his friends.

The angry voices overhead dwindled to one, that of a dominant female with strong views on the efforts of the two men attempting to move Delphi's upright piano to the head of the stairway. Hayes guessed this virago must be the lady of the house.

'Mind the paint, for God's sake!' she shrilled. Delphi darted from Hayes' line of sight and after a further flurry of vicious directions from all sides the older woman was persuaded to come down and leave the way clear for the barrel chested removal men.

Iris Chambers descended like a queen, the wide stairway enhanced by a wrought-iron balustrade, the polished oak treads remaining uncarpeted. Delphi bounced along in her wake, her animation contrasting with the loaded atmosphere like a beam of sunlight shafting a thunderous sky.

The woman held out her hand to Hayes, a wintry smile bypassing her eyes. He introduced himself, flashing his ID for her inspection. A fine looking woman, he decided. Probably late fifties but with the firm chin and even firmer handshake of a woman with no time to waste on niceties.

'My husband is out, Chief Inspector. You should have warned us you were coming. As you can see we've got our hands full here.'

She wore navy trousers and a short kimono jacket, the yellow gleam of an amber necklace echoing hazel eyes which sparked with irritation. Hayes knew how she felt, the two men struggling to manoeuvre the piano reminding him all too well of an old Laurel and Hardy movie in which a piano is let loose down an interminable flight of concrete steps.

Delphi ran back upstairs to remonstrate with the two hefty weightlifters in blue overalls and called on the efforts of a third member of the team hidden by the bulk of the instrument.

Iris pushed Hayes aside at the bottom of the stairs to get a decent view as the men adjusted the straps around the piano and gingerly lowered it down the first few feet.

The dark head of the third member of the gang shot into view, and Hayes recognized Johnny Todd, the piano tuner. Mangled shouts flew in all directions, Iris barely containing her exasperation.

'For Christ's sake watch what you're doing, you oafs. I'll bloody well sue you if you damage the wall.'

Delphi stood beside Johnny, watching the sweating efforts of the team to negotiate a forty degree turn in the stairway.

'Why on earth take the wretched thing to the village at all, Delphi?' Iris bawled. 'Surely you could make do with the piano at the rehearsal rooms.'

Johnny intervened, squeezing past the struggles of his men to adjust the straps and join the heavier of the two at the front. Inch by inch, they edged the piano down, each man streaming with perspiration.

Iris visibly relaxed as another onlooker joined the scene, a slight figure in a denim suit and Prada trainers, trailing a whiff of what Hayes could swear was a spliff in his wake. He draped a languorous arm around his mother's shoulder and pecked her cheek, whispering a remark which caused a smile to break the fierce anxiety at a situation Iris Chambers clearly felt had got out of control.

Hayes and Bellamy stood back, both eyeing their quarry with interest. Young Chambers had the confident mien of the crown prince, his fine bone structure almost too delicate for a man in his thirties. Prison had apparently left him unscathed, although Bellamy privately conjectured that this undersized bloke with the floppy hair must have had a rough time of it in the exercise yard and probably even rougher in the shower block.

The piano was almost there. Everyone held their breath, the atmosphere electric. Johnny directed his team-mate to edge to one side as he adjusted the lower strap but a horrified yell from the man slowing down the descent from the rear broke out. Johnny, bracing himself against the weight as the piano gradually slid sideways and pinned his assistant against the balustrade, stumbled, yelling at the man at the top to hold fast.

Iris moved in just as the strap slid from Johnny's grasp, and with horrific certainty Hayes leapt forward in an effort to snatch her aside as the piano swung, then tottered, then crashed down, the terrible sound of jangling keys and splitting woodwork almost drowning her shriek of terror.

Bellamy tried to haul off the weight but Iris was trapped, her head streaming with blood, her eyes blank as gold coins. Delphi started to scream, the high pitched noise rising above the disaster in a crescendo of fear as she scrambled over the debris, only to be held back by Hayes.

'Bellamy! Quick. Ring for an ambulance. Can we get this bloody piano off her, Johnny?'

Maurice pushed everyone aside to kneel beside his mother. Her face was bloodless, her pelvis trapped under the solid weight of the instrument. The removal men looked stunned, only moving into action as Todd started wrenching at the heap of splintered wood and ironwork jammed between the metal balustrade and the floor. Within minutes they had it off and quickly shoved it away on broken castors to the centre of the hallway, leaving the inert body of Iris Chambers bleeding on to a Persian rug.

Hayes pushed Delphi into a side room and shouted instructions to give the injured woman some air. Maurice hung over her, keening, inconsolable, all his bravura snatched away in a matter of moments. The ambulance arrived, the paramedics making a swift assessment before loading their patient on to a stretcher.

It was all over in what seemed like minutes, the wreckage of the piano bundled out into the van with indecent haste. Johnny Todd looked completely done in, and after the ambulance had sped off with Maurice in attendance, the remaining four assembled in the drawing room.

Delphi and Johnny stared at each other with total disbelief, Hayes taking it upon himself to pour stiff drinks all round.

'Where's your father?' he barked.

'In London. Some sort of motor show, I think.'

'Can you phone him?'

'I'll try.' Her voice was barely audible and Todd looked daggers at Hayes, appalled by his fierce tone. Delphi left the room. Johnny was about to speak when Hayes rounded on him, his eyes blazing.

'And while Miss Chambers is making her phone call I think you have a few questions to answer. From where I was standing, Mr Todd, I fail to understand how this accident could have happened. The straps are undamaged and your men are presumably experienced in this sort of work. You and your incompetent crew may have killed Iris Chambers. A signed statement while your recollection of the sequence of events is clear would be useful, don't you agree?'

It was only later that Hayes remembered the reason he and his sergeant had been at the Old Rectory in the first place. Well, Maurice wasn't going anywhere, was he?

Hayes decided to take the rest of the day off.

Nineteen

Iris Chambers had had a narrow escape.

Hayes phoned the hospital that evening and had a terse exchange with the man in charge, the usual reticent type called Froude who only opened up when Hayes came over all official and mentioned that the exact cause of the apparent accident was under investigation.

'Chief Inspector Hayes, you said? May I ring you back? When I have spoken to Sir Alec.'

Hayes sighed, relinquishing his evening with Radio Three with reluctance, and drove out on to the main road against a strong influx of fancy dressed revellers homing in on a teenage barbeque at the pub on the green. Saturday night off was a bloody mirage, he decided. Policing should carry a health warning: Danger. Social Life and Marriage Seriously in Peril.

The interrupted bulletin from Froude was, in fact, worth the ride. The Chambers op had been a success and the prognosis promised a complete recovery.

'An extremely lucky lady, Chief Inspector. I gather from reports that you yourself probably saved her life. Death By Piano. It would have made a riveting headline.' He sniggered, a snuffly, choked-in rattle hardly qualifying as an expression of congratulation; Hayes could picture a jumped-up hospital administrator chuckling through an apology for a moustache.

'What about her head wound?'

'Superficial cuts and mild concussion. Mrs Chambers is resting comfortably. Her children are with her.'

'And Mr Chambers?'

'Cannot be reached. Away on business, I understand. Any objection to a press release, Chief Inspector? The local people are keen to get the full story.'

'I dare say Chambers Junior will want to be discreet. Play it down, Mr Froude. The family are unlikely to thank anyone for loose talk. Accidents in the home are a familiar story in your A&E department, I'm sure.'

He rang off, toying with the notion of salvaging what was left of the evening. He shuffled through the notes on the Prentice file and phoned Pippa Cooper, WDC Robbins' housemate.

'Roger? A drink at your local in Haddenham? I thought you'd be all tied up on this Chambers business. Jenny's up at the hospital now with that sergeant of yours.'

'Er, yes. Well, actually I'm a bastard when it comes to delegation. How about it then? There's a pretty decent bar menu if you're on.'

He picked her up at the cottage, hooting as the car drew into the kerb, reluctant to make a splash of abducting a resident in Sandy Prentice's village, the usual hotbed of gossip he guessed. In fact, he half convinced himself that dating Pippa Cooper was all in the line of duty: background material?

She slammed her door and jumped into the passenger seat like it was a get-away car, Hayes accelerating off into the darkness with a feeling of elation.

'You all right?' he said. 'A murderer on the loose and then your new lodger's mum brained by a piano? Pretty shattering. I presume Delphi's moved back home?'

He glanced at his companion, her scent powerfully drowning the car interior's latent miasma of cigarette fumes, empty sandwich wrappers and wet shoes. She wore black: black leggings, black polo-neck sweater and little black boots.

Luckily, she had thrown a rust coloured pashmina on top which gave the lie to Hayes' first impression that the evening was likely to be shrouded in gloom. She turned periwinkle blue eyes on him with all the acuity of a laser.

'Me? All right? Of course I'm all right. I feel really bad about the accident though. Poor Delphi. Yeah, she's run back to Daddy. But what about poor Johnny Todd? It won't do his reputation any good, putting butter-fingered louts on the job. But there you go,' she said, grinning at her surprise date, 'life's full of little surprises.'

Hayes put his foot down and headed straight back to Haddenham, parking by the village pond, pointing out the lighted windows of his flat above the butcher's.

'My butcher friend likes the local rascals to think I'm at home nights,' he said in response to her raised eyebrow. 'He had a few break-ins before I moved in, regards me like some sort of rottweiler. I live alone. Divorced, in case you're wondering. No kids, no pets, very little furniture and a sizable overdraft. OK?'

'Nice to know who I'm sharing a bottle of wine with. I'm assuming the evening's off duty, right?'

'Strictly ballroom,' he replied, steering her into the rosy atmosphere of the saloon. They settled at a corner table, Hayes shedding his seemingly permanently soaked raincoat and padding off to the bar. The barbeque party was at full volume in the pub garden. The next half-hour moved smoothly towards the contemplation of the menu, and after ordering two plates of steak and chips they settled into second gear.

'And Iris is going to be OK? You're sure? From what Jenny said before your sergeant whisked her off to sit by the bedside with Delphi and that brother of hers, I imagined it was practically curtains.'

'Well, it's going to take a few weeks to mend but ultimately I'm assured a bit of a limp will be the worst of it.'

'Why did you send Jenny to sit in?'

'Nosy thing, aren't you? I thought this was supposed to be my night off!'

'You're keeping tabs on Maurice I bet.' She sipped her wine, eyeing him with blatant curiosity.

'Why d'you say that?'

'Everyone knows he's been in prison. Give a dog a bad name. I bet he'd cop a bloody fortune if his mother croaked. He's the favourite, you know, Delphi's Daddy's girl.' She paused. 'You're not thinking Morry had something to do with the accident, are you?'

'Christ, woman, with an imagination like yours you should be in showbusiness, not the music lark. On that score, how about the Brandt concert next weekend? Will Delphi be able to accompany? She was all but shot to pieces by the accident. Blames herself, I dare say, moving the piano being at her insistence.'

Pippa shook her head, nonplussed. 'Who knows? We shall have to have her assurance by Monday. Brandt's arriving for a run through on Wednesday and my boss has got him booked up for various publicity shots running up to the festival.'

'Well, it'll prove one way or another whether Delphi's a real professional. As her mother's on the mend I can't see why she should cancel. There's her brother doing nothing – he could do the hospital visiting, no problem.'

'Half-brother.'

'What?'

'Half-brother. Iris was married before. When she got her hooks into Noel he was married too. They met at the office. Usual story – pretty secretary, boss bored with selling cars. Inevitable really.'

'Chambers was already married? Had children?'

'No. Iris was the one with the kid. This is all old history. My auntie in Oxford was working at Chambers Autos herself at the time. And in those days office love-ins were a terrible scandal, not like today when practically anything goes so long as the boss isn't accused of sexual harassment. Iris got herself pregnant, waltzes off with Noel, marries him and produces Delphi who's the light of his life. He adopted Maurice and brought him up as his own, posh boarding school, the lot. But Iris propelling her son into the business is all a front – a bad lad. Well, not really bad I suppose. Just weak, spoiled by Iris, bullied by Noel and upstaged in beauty and brains by his little sister.'

'Is all this generally known?'

'Pretty well. The talk goes round and round in a small firm like Chambers, not helped by Iris being so damned efficient. Noel owes her a lot. Iris wangled her way from secretary to office manager to wife and ultimately owner in all but name. And she deserves it. The business has flourished since she moved in and it doesn't stop there. After they bought the Old Rectory Iris Chambers made up her mind to move in on the social set round here, to be a big frog in this little pond, God knows why – the ultimate challenge, I suppose. She's put a whole bundle of Chambers' money into elbowing into the dinner-party circuit and with energy like hers she soon muscled in on the snobby big-wigs, splashed out on the local jubilee celebrations, set up an old people's lunch club in the village hall, put herself on the parish church council – you name it. The nobs at Kelvin Court, Lady Honora and Major Vennor, turn a blind eye. They know the people round here aren't taken in. The locals grab the cash and doff their caps to the gentry same as always. Iris has too much push, that's her trouble. She can't see it but to give the poor woman her due she deserves everything she's got.'

'Even Maurice?'

Pippa giggled. 'No one deserves Maurice. Hey, what about that bit about showing me your etchings at the flat after this?'

'Never said anything about etchings, my sweet. But I've got a terrific line in CDs.'

Twenty

Next morning Hayes spoke with his sergeant about the vigil at Mrs Chambers' hospital bedside.

'Well, if you think Maurice is unlikely to do a bunk, Bellamy – and I hardly think he will abandon Iris while he still thinks he's in the clear – shall we leave the WPCs to hold the fort? They can make a note of comings and goings, keep an ear to the keyhole when the missing husband turns up.'

'He's back, sir. Turned up just after breakfast. Lucky bloke almost talked his way out of it, his wife being so groggy, but Maurice gave him a right earful. Chambers was supposed to be at this motor show but no one could contact him and he wasn't spending Saturday night at his hotel either. Told his missus he'd been invited to go and see some new premises of one of the other dealers, stayed on for lunch, got too pissed to go back to the show and booked into his club in the West End. Only got the message about the accident when he got back to his hotel Sunday morning to pack, so he says.'

Hayes laughed. 'Might even be true.'

'Jenny Robbins went off duty at eight and one of the others took over. The Chambers lot are not happy with the surveillance but the hospital administrator has assured them it's new policy – to keep an eye on any patient until the police complete statements about suspicious accidents. Noel Chambers assumes we're hunting for evidence against that piano tuner chap, and Maurice is dead keen to be cast as the good guy for a change, so we may be able to keep the lid on it for a day or two until Mrs Chambers is transferred to a private hospital and well enough to make a statement. Her husband insists on it.'

'Is that likely so soon?'

'The surgeon is against any immediate move, of course, but the lady is already demanding to go home. She hates hospitals, Chambers says, and it strikes me that if she says "Jump", he jumps.'

'Well, keep me posted. Set up a watch team and I'll ring you later. I'm going back to the Prentice house to check a few points – I can't help feeling we're missing something somewhere, Bellamy. Make sure that dossier on Maurice Chambers is on my desk first thing tomorrow, including a mug shot from the files. I'm going to London in the morning: the solicitor put me on to a couple of leads I'd like to follow up.'

The sun was shining for a change, a crisp fall in temperature sharpening the scent of burning leaves as he parked his car next to the disused barn at the edge of the field overlooking Didcot Drive. A thin column of smoke issued from one of the gardens and wafted across the stubble field like skeins of blue silk. Hayes pushed through a barrier of nettles and prickly scrub to have a look at the barn.

In fact it wasn't a barn at all. The basic structure was a couple of railway carriages roofed over by strips of corrugated iron to form what must at one time have been a sheep pen of sorts. The place was long abandoned, the windows smashed and the doors hanging loose, the remains of a camp fire now fallen into ashes suggesting the place had recently been used as a kids' den or a tramps' stopover. Inside, the wreckage was almost complete, two plastic beer crates and a broken chair having served as seating. Hayes grinned, imagining the fun the village boys must have had in this hideout, a perfect gang headquarters. Or maybe kids no longer played such games? Clearly it was no lovers' trysting place, rat holes all too evident to put off the girls. He poked about in some rancid straw and unearthed three empty whisky bottles and some discarded lager tins but otherwise the place seemed innocent enough.

He stared out at the houses on the horizon. Didcot Drive was hardly more than three hundred yards across the field and the muddy footpath passed like an arrow linking the older part of Newton Greys with the cul-de-sac. Hayes stood lost in thought, contemplating the possibility of a stalker with binoculars having a distinct view of Sandy Prentice's back garden. Had he jumped to the wrong conclusion in assuming the killer was someone familiar with the dead woman, a local man?

He tried to push this unwanted conjecture aside. A stranger to the village ogling a good looking woman careless about closing the blinds at night? A woman whose antics in the conservatory had inflamed the sexual fantasies of a passing weirdo? Such a person was totally out of his line of enquiry and could make the hunt for Sandy's murderer almost impossible . . .

He changed his plan of action and set off in the opposite direction towards the Old Rectory and, keeping well away from the direct route, skirted the pub car park and arrived at the house in less than fifteen minutes. This way made an interesting tour of what would seem to be the back-side of Newton Greys, skimming the allotments adjoining the school and finally crossing the lane which ultimately continued past Pippa Cooper's house.

He was getting to know the village at last, his first impression of the new housing developments on the far side sharpened he wryly suspected, by the evening he had spent with the girl from Holly Cottage. Pippa was one of those people who seem perpetually on the verge of laughter, her response to Hayes' smart-talk prevarication being amusement rather than the uncertainty a date with Roger Hayes usually engendered. He was attracted by her confidence, a shared delight in chamber music being a bonus he readily accepted as pretty amazing. The passing encounters he had had since the divorce, had been more of the 'big tits, no brains' variety. He shut out these random thoughts, wondering if he was becoming more fearful of any relationship than need be. Patsy Hayes had left him unsure of himself when it came to picking winners.

The Old Rectory stood well back from the road, screened from the church by a high wall. As he walked up the drive the sound of church bells rang out. He glanced at his watch. Nearly eleven. A call to Morning Prayer, a reminder to the backsliders that the Reverend Harcourt would be counting heads and probably giving his parishioners a fierce sermon on the virtues of Love Thy Neighbour, their own tragic neighbour having lain dead for nearly a fortnight and no one in this self-styled 'close community' having missed her. Perhaps some kind person would light a candle for Sandy Prentice? Perhaps the Reverend Harcourt would lead his congregation in a prayer for her soul?

Hayes knocked loudly, the sound ploughing through the notes of a serious piano practice cascading through the open window of what he remembered as the drawing room. Yesterday's terrible accident still jarred, his arrival with Bellamy to question Maurice Chambers about his association with Sandy swept aside by events: a piano precipitated downstairs and almost killing Iris Chambers. Yet another mystery. He had been there, for heaven's sake, standing practically shoulder to shoulder with the poor woman. Was it really a stupid accident? Was Iris the real target? Was Johnny Todd so inexperienced that he had loosened the straps at a vital moment, thus forcing his crew to lose control? But with a murder inquiry on hand, the Chambers piano fiasco would just have to wait.

He banged again with no response and discovered that the door was, in fact, on the latch. He walked in.

'Hello? Delphi? May I come through?'

At last his arrival registered. The pounding of the keyboard ceased abruptly and Delphine Chambers looked up as he entered the room. She looked deathly pale, her hair wild, a faint bloom of sweat glistening on her upper lip. She rose, opening her hands in a gesture of confusion.

He pressed on. 'Forgive me barging in like this – you're still in shock, I imagine. Your father's at the hospital now – I expect you've heard . . .'

'Um, yes. Of course . . . He rang me from town. My mother's responding terrifically well.' She smiled wanly. 'She has the constitution of an ox. Look, why don't you come through? I'll make some coffee. I could do with a break.'

She led him down a flagged passage and through a baize door to the kitchen where a middle-aged party in a flowery apron was rolling out pastry.

'Ah, Mrs Drake, this is Inspector – er, sorry, I've forgotten your surname.'

'Chief Inspector Hayes. I was here yesterday.'

'Good gracious! You pulled Mrs Chambers out of the way, saved her from certain death so I heard. It was my weekend off – went over to Abingdon on the bus to stay with my sister. And when I heard—'

'Yes, Mrs Drake, it was very good of you to rush back, we all appreciate it, but the inspector has a lot to do. Perhaps I could make some coffee as you're so busy with lunch.'

'Don't you bother your 'ead, Delphi. I can pop along with a tray to the drawing room in two shakes.'

'That would be lovely.' Delphi pushed him out, whispering urgently to leave the kitchen to the help who, Hayes guessed had her work cut out keeping tabs on the motley crew who made up the Chambers household: a bossy lady of the house, an employer who wafted in and out with apparently acceptable absences, a useless son who had lately been in prison and a nervy young musician who was struggling to make a career for herself in a world crowded with genius. And he thought he had a difficult job!

They settled back in the drawing room and struggled with Delphi's recollections of the accident. She lay on the sofa like some highly strung creature exhausted by the tribulations that crowded in on all sides. The housekeeper bustled in with a tray then left and closed the door behind her.

'Shall you be able to play for Brandt?'

'Of course. My agent would kill me if I let him down – if there was anything left of me after Pippa had had a go.' The jest was grim and Hayes sipped his coffee, regarding the girl with sympathy. He was not entirely in tune with any member of the Chambers' family, he decided, though Noel might prove to be a nice ordinary bloke, a man surrounded by strong personalities who sought only to relax somewhere else, possibly with someone less controlling than Iris.

'You do have other professional engagements, I assume?'

Delphi winced. 'Not much. I've accompanied Florian Brandt before so it wasn't too difficult persuading him to accept me for the festival. But he has his own accompanist for the London concerts and some important venues in Birmingham and Edinburgh. Are you familiar with his work? I remember you were enthusiastic when we all had supper together in Thame, and Pippa mentioned you had studied music yourself in another life, pre sleuthing. Fancy that! A cultured copper!' She giggled.

Hayes swiftly snuffed out this line of small talk and insisted on returning to her recollection of the accident. They discussed it at length but nothing new surfaced, Delphi vehemently defending Johnny Todd's actions.

'I've explained it all to Daddy. He's more than happy that it was just a dreadful mischance. Take no notice of anything

Maurice has to say – he's got it in for me lately and anyone connected with me.'

'Why's that?'

She shrugged, jumping to her feet and ranging round the room, stroking the piano as she passed and eventually coming to rest framed in the sunlight streaming through the long windows.

'We're a bit old for sibling rivalry but Morry was first-born. I came later and he resented all the fuss. I can understand that, but he's not a little boy any longer. Maurice resents my father's preference for me, which unfortunately has become all too obvious since Maurice was released and came back here to live. He plays them off against each other, my parents. They quarrel. My mother is a powerful character, but Maurice manipulates everyone. He's my brother and I love him but I have no illusions about him. He would do anything to be shot of Daddy and me, a split in the marriage would suit him nicely. But there's the business . . . Mother won't give up the firm and her status in the county is important to her. She started work as a single parent and jealously guards her place in what she calls "local society", not easy since Maurice blotted the family name. It's difficult for an outsider to understand, but if she and Daddy break up, Mother will fight tooth and nail to keep what she feels is her own. Maurice needs her. And if it means he ends up in the original twosome that suits him just fine. I'm piggy in the middle in all this – one reason I'm trying to move away, to be independent. This accident came just when I almost got away.'

'Not very far.'

'Far enough.'

Hayes stood, placing his cup on the tray, and held out his hand. 'I won't interrupt your practice any longer. I came to examine the staircase and to clarify things in my mind. May I wander round? Get the feel of things?'

'Of course. But please, don't blame Johnny. It will ruin him if word gets out that he's dangerously bungled a job. He runs a sideline moving concert grands. They're usually rented by concert halls, you know. Soloists require such high standards that they insist on seasoned instruments from specialists. Johnny is a sort of middleman, knows all the right people and uses the best team available when he has a private removal job. Johnny Todd is the best, believe me.'

Hayes took his leave and quietly closed the door, the strains of a Chopin polonaise sifting through the house as he pursued his walkabout.

He left through a back passage where a row of waxed jackets and mackintoshes hung on hooks above a neat row of outdoor boots and shoes. He bent down to inspect a pair of hiking boots, turning them over to examine the unusual pattern of the sole. In a moment of exhilaration he carried his booty back to the car and stowed the boots in an evidence bag.

Twenty-one

Hayes idled through the Monday morning rush hour in south London, wondering if it would have been quicker to take the train, but at least the traffic jams gave him time to mull over his lack of progress.

The Superintendent was getting edgy, threatening to appear on a crime watch TV show, a matter on which they disagreed. Hayes held strongly to the view that if the murder of Sandy Prentice was a parochial crime limited to within a five-mile radius of Newton Greys, any local with a clue would have come forward before. The delay in reporting even a minor observation would only have aggravated the anxieties of someone who had denied to the police any insider knowledge which might have helped the investigation or, if proved malicious, leave what was already a hotbed of suspicion with rancorous speculation all round the village which would probably deter any new informant.

The used-car showroom was an extensive affair decked out with bunting and huge placards advertising Autumn Sale Bargains. He parked behind the office and strolled amongst the expensive metalwork on display. This was no bargain basement, the vehicles on sale being in the top range with prices to match. A salesman sidled up, smooth as silk.

'Anything special you have in mind, sir?'

Hayes smiled and silently produced his warrant card, which swiftly sobered the encounter.

'I'd like to speak to the manager. My sergeant was here last week regarding a sale which interests us. I'll go through to the office, shall I?'

'Mr Blackwood's out on business.'

'His secretary will do.'

The man reluctantly nodded and led the way to an office tastefully fitted with chromium and leather like an Italian shoe shop.

The girl in the office was the sort Hayes warmed to: slick as paint and efficient with it. She wore an emerald green trouser suit and jangly gold bangles, and a narrow pair of spectacles on her pert little nose did nothing but enhance the impression of a girl with her wits about her. A picture flashed through his mind: Iris Chambers must have been a smart cookie just like this young woman when she first arrived at Chambers Autos to work in Noel's sales office.

He explained his business, confirming that Paula Phillips was the girl who had remembered the sale of the MG to Sandy Prentice and signed a statement to that effect.

'Tony here remembers too, he was the one who steered her away from a Volvo the bloke she was with wanted her to have.'

'Too boring for a sexy looking piece like that – she wanted something snazzy, something to catch the eye at traffic lights. Know what I mean?'

'But the guy wanted to get her into something a bit less noticeable?'

'A right wet blanket he was. But she wasn't having any of it. Mind you, he knew his nuts and bolts, went over that motor with a nit comb, took me out on a trial run an' all. I was holding on to my belly before he'd finished.'

'Boy racer type? You recall this transaction that well, with all the hundreds of sales you've made since last year?'

'I bloody do as it 'appens,' he retorted. 'Paid in fifties – even here that's rare.'

'But it was her choice? Her car?'

The girl chipped in, all smiles. 'Quite fancied him myself – too young for her. The poor woman got murdered, so the sergeant said.'

Hayes produced a couple of pictures of Maurice, one a mug shot which did him no favours and the other a cutting from the *Oxford Mail* showing him with his father presenting a cheque to a local school to pay for a new gymnasium. Iris stood next to the Mayor, looking like a politician who's just got in with a thumping great majority.

They signed a fresh statement identifying Maurice as the man brought along to give Sandy expert advice which she had rejected. Hayes wasn't surprised. He couldn't picture the Prentice lady behind the wheel of a staid saloon such as the one Maurice wanted her to buy.

He declined coffee and shook hands all round, keen to be across the city to Paddington to suss out Sandy's former flatmate if she was at home. He should have driven up to town on Sunday, caught the girl on her day off, but combining the car showroom with another couple of calls appealed to his need to avoid wasting two trips and at least pinning Maurice down to a closer relationship with Sandy than he was prepared to volunteer was another small nail in the man's coffin. But nosing round Sandy's lifestyle was not getting him anywhere when it came down to it. The salesman shot over to a browsing customer and Hayes disappeared behind the office block to reclaim his car.

He was unlocking the door when he felt a touch on his arm. It was Paula, the office totty, looking nervously over her shoulder.

'Yes?' He leaned against the car, eyeing the girl with renewed interest. Her demeanour had changed entirely, her eyes now scanning the forecourt with the anxiety of a shoplifter.

'Look, Inspector. There's something I didn't tell your

sergeant before. I didn't think it important and besides,' she said, choosing her words with care, 'Tony would have gone berserk if he'd found out. See, it was like this. After the mechanic bloke left with the woman who got stabbed, he phoned me up. Asked me for a date. I saw no harm in it – Tony don't own me, we're not engaged nor nothin'. This guy took me to a couple of nice clubs and we had a great time and I was getting really interested. But then he stopped phoning, just like he'd dropped off the edge of the world. All this was about a year ago, see?' She shrugged. 'I'd gone off him a bit anyway – he was a terrible dancer.'

Hayes pulled her closer, his words brisk as a wire brush. 'His name?'

'He said, "Call me Bambi." On account of his nice blue eyes, he reckoned. I never got much out of him about his job nor nothin' and we just took taxis so I never found out where he lived. But he was always free with wads of cash and who was I to turn down a date like that?'

'Did you ask him about the woman?'

'He said she was the girlfriend of a mate of his who asked him to see her right with the car. Bambi was a bloody good car mechanic, make no mistake. Tony said he even had to do a deal over some touching up Bambi had spotted on the rear bumper.'

'You didn't tell anyone about this?'

'Not likely! Tony's a malicious bugger. Would have caused ructions with the boss if he'd found out I'd been doing a number with one of the customers.'

'But Bambi wasn't the paying customer, was he?'

She shrugged, unwilling to get in any deeper. 'I should have told your sergeant but you can see how it is . . . Can you keep this confidential? My job'd be on the line if you make it official that I'd been holding out.'

Hayes patted her arm. 'No sweat. Just a private little chat

between ourselves, Paula. Makes identifying my suspect that much easier, that's all.'

'He 'asn't done nothin', has he? You're not putting Bambi in the frame for killing that poor woman?'

'Just background stuff, Paula. Nothing heavy. Thanks anyway. Don't lose any sleep over this, it's just between ourselves, OK?'

He drove off leaving her standing in the back lot with all the scruffy cars awaiting glamour makeovers.

Finding Sandy's former flat was a piece of cake and, like the solicitor had said, the area was distinctly up-market. A porter rang through to alert her flatmate, a Miss Buxton it would seem, and Hayes stood in the air freshened lift listening to the soothing muzak normally only heard in a hotel elevator.

Miss Buxton was a surprise: a big black girl with eyes like prunes and the graceful stance of an Egyptian figure carved from basalt. She examined Hayes' ID with interest and finally admitted him to a sitting room overlooking the square.

Twenty-two

He got back late, just catching the Superintendent as he was about to leave to attend a Masonic get-together. Anxious to hear Hayes out, Supt Waller checked his watch, phoned through to his driver and agreed to give Hayes fifteen minutes.

Hayes pitched straight in, describing the salient points. 'And finally I want to bring in Maurice Chambers for questioning.'

Waller looked glum, Hayes' methods leaving him anxious about flimsy evidence, a criticism that had tagged his new chief inspector ever since the Crowne case, an investigation which had ended badly and had precipitated Hayes' transfer to Waller's little fiefdom. A tangle with the Chambers clan, an influential local family like the Crownes, was the last thing he wanted. Even so, the Prentice murder was beginning to attract attention and once the expert evidence from the entomologist – the Maggot Man, as Waller dubbed him – was exposed to scrutiny at the inquest who knew what publicity would follow? In Waller's estimation none of it would be good. Their main advantage was that Morry Chambers had form, a fact which even Noel Chambers could not deny. He jotted down some notes and sighed, leaning back heavily, regarding Hayes with narrowed gaze.

'Right, mate, on your head be it. Get Chambers in here first thing – and try to do the job with some sort of discretion, none of your bull-in-a-china-shop routines. We don't want to be accused of harassment, you know what these civil liberties people are like. When are these hiking boots likely to be available from Forensics?'

'I said it was urgent. I'll have confirmation before I go after Chambers.'

'His mother's still pretty sick, I hear. Not likely to cause problems, I hope? She's not in intensive care, is she, likely to take a nosedive when her boy's lifted?'

Hayes slyly touched wood under the desk. 'No, sir, no chance of that. In fact she wants to go home, says she hates hospitals and is trying to get herself discharged on the understanding that twenty-four hour nursing care will be on tap at the Old Rectory.'

Hayes accompanied his boss to the forecourt, raising a half-salute as Waller's car sped off to Oxford. He left instructions with the officer on duty and spent the next hour in his office writing up the background information he had gleaned from doorstepping the glamorous Miss Buxton at Sandy's former residence.

Cindy Buxton, age twenty-four, model, Flat 16, Porchester House, London W2. Occupied the accommodation for only three months, renting from a Mrs Carberry who lives in the penthouse suite in the same building.

Hayes paused, recalling the extraordinary encounter with the two women. Miss Buxton, as he persisted in addressing her despite her cheerful invitation to 'Call me Cindy, everyone does,' excused herself after a few minutes, pleading a hairdressing appointment.

'But I'll call Mrs Carberry, shall I? Ask her to come down and speak with you? She's been expecting a call from the police ever since we read about poor Sandy's murder.'

'That would be very helpful if it's convenient. As a recent tenant, Miss Buxton, you would not have known

Mrs Prentice of course. Mrs Carberry may be able to supply the information I need.'

The girl span round. 'What d'you mean, me not knowing Sandy? Of course I knew her. Not well, but we shared this flat for weeks after Samantha, one of the other girls, moved back to Edinburgh to be with her kid.'

'Are you saying Mrs Prentice lived here since you moved in? She kept on her flat share after she moved to her new house?'

'Of course she did. How could she work from that place? "My little cottage in the country", she used to call it, though from the pictures in the papers it looked no better than a flash council house to me.'

Cindy Buxton was clearly no country lover. She phoned Mrs Carberry and departed just as soon as her landlady arrived at the door.

The relationship between the two women was odd, Mrs Carberry dismissing Cindy with barely a nod. After examining Hayes' warrant card she settled down on the sofa next to him and lit a cigarette.

'Now, what's all this about, Chief Inspector?'

After this brisk beginning Hayes' trusted interview technique seemed to lose pace, the woman confronting him being in no way fazed by the close questioning of a senior police officer.

'I was given to understand Mrs Prentice no longer used this flat, had moved out some time ago, according to her solicitor.'

'Ah well,' she said, drawing steadily on her king size cigarette. 'Sandy was a close one and no mistake. We'd been friends for ages – met, when Sandy had a little job in a Knightsbridge salon I used to go to many years ago before she went freelance.'

'Then you would be familiar with her hairdressing contracts with nursing homes?'

'Oh yes. Sandy enjoyed her work with the patients, refused to give it up though naturally she had no need to continue.'

'She had private means? An inheritance?'

She laughed. 'You mean Sandy's old story about an aunt leaving her money? No way, Inspector. Sandy earned every penny herself, and good luck to her. We weren't just friends, we were business partners.'

Hayes tried to disguise his confusion but the woman in the designer suit and pearls the size of cherries smiled encouragingly, patting his arm in a gesture which was almost pitying.

'You don't get it, do you, dear? Sandy and I had our own little money-spinner. The hairdressing lark was practically a hobby for her, a social thing, her little way of keeping her feet on the ground. Sandy was a lovely girl, all heart. God rot the bastard who did that to her.'

'I'm afraid you've lost me, Mrs Carberry. Please, just explain your connection with the deceased.'

She stubbed out her cigarette and frowned, regarding him with mild exasperation.

'This flat is mine, together with two others in the building which I let to my girls. I retired from business some years ago and Sandy and I decided to go legit. We started up an introduction agency – you know the sort of thing, putting saddos in touch with other saddos and hoping that some of them at least would finish up at the altar.' She laughed, touching Hayes' hand in a gesture of complicity. 'It failed. We lost a bundle of money on that little venture, so we had another think and came up with Valentine's.'

She crossed the room, took a business card from a silver cigarette box and handed it to him.

'"Valentine Escorts,"' he read. '"A Superior Service for Superior People." The girls use these flats for prostitution?' he said stiffly.

Her guffaw rang out harshly, spiking his pomposity.

'I'm not that stupid! What do you take me for, darling? No. Valentine's is a kosher escort agency for businessmen who like a little company in their free time. They arrange to meet their escorts at hotels, of course, and I insist my girls are beautifully turned out and behave like débutantes. Discreet enquiries are made – I wouldn't like my employees to face any unpleasantness – but such introductions are a respectable part of the leisure industry.' It all sounded remarkably businesslike.

'But what they get up to with clients at the end of the evening is no concern of Valentine's?'

She shrugged. 'These flats are let on very special terms, no paying gentlemen callers you could say, though boyfriends are OK if they're off the premises before breakfast. That's why I always put two girls in together, usually one novice with one of my seniors. It's convenient for them to have somewhere central, somewhere to keep their nice clothes. Some of my girls have homes of their own elsewhere, of course, and only rent from me on short leases. But Sandy would always need a *pied-à-terre* in town, taking that awful house way out in the sticks was a silly gesture. She was planning to get married, you know, wanted to put on a domestic front to reel in that slippery bastard.'

'You met him?'

'No. Sandy and I were pals but she was always a very private person, liked to play her cards very close to her chest.'

'Did she mention his name?'

'No, never. But I got the impression there was a hitch. She said she would let me buy her out of Valentine's when the time came, but it was all pie in the sky as far as I could see. I suspect he was stringing her along. She liked younger men, you know. "Sandy's Toyboys", I used to call them. She had a special way with the shy ones. She did gigs for Valentine's you know. Right up to the end.'

'She took clients herself?'

'Sure. Why not? I used to pull her leg about it. The other girls called her the Geisha Momma.'

'Why was that?'

'Geishas are professional cock teasers. All for plumping up the punters' egos but no more. She was popular. I had regulars who asked for Sandy specially. Nice blokes, all ages, men who liked a lively night out with no strings attached. Sandy was brilliant at it.'

'Names? The names of the men who took her out regularly?'

Maureen Carberry raised a pencilled brow. 'We use nicknames, Chief Inspector. No labels are necessary and even if I knew, and I don't, it would wreck my business to blab to the police, wouldn't it?'

Hayes admitted defeat and, after staring round at the room with the air of a man who had run out of options, rose to go. He paused as she held open the door for him.

'Just one more thing, Mrs Carberry. We have been unable to trace any next-of-kin. But Mrs Prentice had a special affection for an old lady called O'Brien. Did she ever mention her to you?'

She shook her head. 'Sandy never spoke of any family. Perhaps this O'Brien person was one of her hairdressing clients?'

He took his leave with a feeling there were things left unsaid, matters on which Sandy Prentice's closest friend was being less than honest.

Hayes drew a line under his notes and turned to the file on Maurice Chambers Bellamy had left on his desk. He totted up the points. Not nearly enough to make a charge stick, unless the ex-con felt like clearing his conscience. Fat chance! His bitter response to this unlikely scenario literally gave him the gripes, reminding him that missing lunch had been a mistake, and missing out on Happy Hour at his local in Haddenham could only be corrected by something in the pie and a pint category before nightfall.

He turned out the lights and pushed off home.

Twenty-three

Maurice Chambers was wheeled into the interview room just after ten the next day. He looked like shit, his tan yellowish, his eyes bloodshot and the shoulder-length hair as stringy as yesterday's spaghetti.

Hayes seated himself next to Bellamy and regarded the sad sack slumped on the seat opposite with weary resignation. Only Maurice's startling blue eyes reflected a spark of interest in proceedings that seemed all too familiar to him. Hayes supposed his stretch inside had left the poor bastard with an enduring inertia when it came to police questioning.

Bellamy switched on the recording machine and ran through the official procedure, finally asking if a solicitor would be required.

Maurice smiled, a sly grimace, and said, 'Why would I need a brief? I haven't done anything.'

Hayes launched into the interrogation, careful to phrase his questions in as non-committal a manner as he could muster.

'Mr Chambers. As you know, we are investigating the murder of Sandra Prentice, who died on the fourth of October in her home.'

'So?'

'You were friends.' It was not a question.

Maurice agreed, and, leaning back, extracted a cigarette packet from the pocket of his jeans and lit up. This pause in proceedings jarred like the ticking of a clock but Hayes quietly gestured to Bellamy to back off, the sergeant all too clearly disapproving of the kid-gloves manner in which the boss was handling their suspect.

'So you agree that a certain relationship existed between the deceased and yourself. Would you care to describe that relationship?'

Maurice squinted at the glowing tip of his cigarette, raising his eyes only to answer. 'No, I wouldn't.'

Hayes sighed, nodding at Bellamy, who launched a more abrasive tone.

'You have frequently been seen depositing empty bottles in the recycling bin outside the village hall.'

Maurice laughed. 'Yeah. I'm a tidy sort of bloke. I thought you coppers had more to worry about than keeping surveillance on a rubbish bin.'

'Your fingerprints are recorded as being found on a bottle of expensive champagne dumped in the period we are interested in. There is a witness who recognizes the bottle as one seen in Sandy Prentice's house the day before she died.' Bellamy was finding it hard to get through, Maurice regarding the sergeant with a degree of what could only be described as dumb insolence. 'Were you in the habit of sharing a bottle of Bollinger with the lady?'

'Regrettably, hardly a habit, sarge, but often enough, if that's what you're after.'

Hayes butted in. 'You were also seen in the vicinity of Didcot Drive on the afternoon of the murder and it would be reasonable to assume that you had been with Mrs Prentice. OK? We are trying to establish a pattern of events here, sir, and your contribution would be useful.'

Maurice stubbed out his cigarette, eyeing Hayes with guarded approval.

'OK. Yes, Sandy and I were pals. Since my release I've been put in an alcohol free zone at home. Despite my objections my father paid an exorbitant amount for a chi-chi detox programme.'

'It was a condition of your returning home?'

'I suppose so. I was in no position to argue the toss with Dad if I wanted to keep my place in the pecking order at the garage.'

'Drink driving being hardly the best recommendation,' Bellamy cut in.

Hayes continued, his quiet words seeming to defuse the artificiality of the situation.

'But you continue to drink privately?'

'I'm no alki, Hayes. Sandy used to work at the clinic and we hit it off straight away. She couldn't see why a fellow my age should be treated like a kid caught with an alco-pop in his back pocket. I wasn't in the same league as the others.'

'Did your parents know about this? Your drinking with this woman you'd met while in rehab?'

'My father found out but he tried to keep it from Mum.'

'Because of the booze, or the woman? A woman of experience who perhaps Mrs Chambers considered an unsuitable friend for her son, an ordinary hairdresser, living at the wrong end of the village?'

Maurice shrugged. 'Partly. Mum was always a terrible snob, of course, but Sandy wasn't the only girl to get up her nose as far as I was concerned.'

'It must have been difficult for you. Living at home, watched at work, never having a place of your own to relax in.'

'You've put your finger on it there. Sandy let me drop in any time, no hassle, and she understood I needed a drink now and then to blur the edges.'

'Financially you are dependent on the good will of your parents?' Bellamy put in.

'For the time being, yeah, sure. An ex-con isn't on any shortlist for the sort of jobs I'm interested in. I've been brought up on the understanding the garages will eventually be mine – and why not?'

'You are an excellent car mechanic for a start,' Hayes said admiringly.

'Where d'you hear that?'

'Actually, Bambi, a girlfriend of yours, Paula, was very enthusiastic about your technical know-how.'

Maurice stiffened.

'Look, Maurice, can we get down to business? Get all this out on the table so you can get back to the hospital? How is Mrs Chambers by the way – improving I hope?'

Hayes' use of 'Bambi' had put a different complexion on the interview and Bellamy moved in on their quarry.

'You took Sandy along to the showroom in the Old Kent Road and checked out her car, didn't you? Don't let's waste any more time on this, mate, we've got signed statements to prove it. You don't want to have to line up on any identity parade, do you?'

Maurice stared at Bellamy, who was grinning like a man who had hit the jackpot.

'OK, sergeant. Yeah, Sandy asked me to go along for the ride. What's wrong with that?'

'Nothing at all,' Bellamy retorted. 'What worries us is, who really put up the cash? Passed over a bloody great wad of fifties with your very own hot little hands, I hear. Looks bad, Morry, if you're making out that poor cow was merely a drinking partner.'

'I've got money!'

Hayes let this go. 'Right. If you're saying you paid for the car it puts a different angle on your claim that you and Sandy were just good pals, doesn't it? Was it, in fact, her own money and you were her agent? If it was just a smokescreen making it look like you were the boyfriend with the open wallet, what was your side of the bargain? I must warn you, Chambers, I've a witness who is willing to swear he has seen you driving that car on at least one occasion. Was the deal a promise that you could borrow her car whenever you needed a ride? The spare keys have never turned up and my witness isn't burdened with a police record, a fact which would, sadly for you, sway opinion his way if it came to it.'

Maurice relaxed. 'I know who you're talking about and it's all lies. That family have had a vendetta against me since that kid died. It was an accident, I panicked and I've paid the price. Local gossip wouldn't stand up in court for a moment, Hayes, and you know it.'

Bellamy looked rattled, peering into his notebook as if it were a crystal ball.

'Right, let's assume you paid all or part of the cost of the MG, and it was registered in Sandy's name on the understanding you could use it whenever you wanted. Was that the reason you tried to persuade her to go for something less stylish, something like a Volvo for instance?'

'Hayes, you're barking up the wrong tree. I lost my licence, I'm in no position to use anyone's car and even if that was the deal with Sandy the arrangement would be impractical – I'm too well known round here and Sandy Prentice wasn't so interested in me she'd share her motor.'

'Let's move on. When I was last at your house I removed this pair of hiking boots from the back passage.' Hayes produced the evidence bag from behind his chair and placed it on the table.

Maurice stared at the boots with interest but no sign of alarm.

'They're yours?'

'Possibly. Lakeland boots are hardly top price gear, Hayes. They're sold in every camping shop in Oxford, for starters.'

'Medium size, Morry. I've been looking at your feet – a bit on the small side for a man. Care to show me your shoes?' Bellamy leaned down and examined Maurice's trainers.

'I'll tell you something to put in your bloody notebook, sergeant. If your boss stole them from our boot rack, they're Delphi's. She's got feet like kippers and the boots by the back door are used by anyone who wants them. Even Mrs Drake uses her boots to put out the washing when the ground's wet. Delphi wears them, I wear them, the housekeeper wears them and if you look around you'll find half the students in Oxford have a pair. They're waterproof and light. Even the bloody piano tuner was wearing them when he was chucking the piano down the stairs!'

'Trouble is, these particular boots bear soil traces linked to the crime scene. And a muddy footprint in the Prentice conservatory matches up perfectly. You were seen on the afternoon in question and you admit you wear the boots.'

Hayes decided the damned boots were proving something of a red herring but Maurice had been flicked on the raw and his eyes sparked with venom as he rose to go.

'You can't keep me here, Hayes. All this eyewash about me barging into Sandy's conservatory in my muddy boots doesn't ring true for a moment. Sandy asked me round for a drink that afternoon you're on about. I walked over the field and left my boots outside as usual. There was no reason to barge in and if you'd known the woman you'd know she would have been seriously pissed off if I'd dragged mud into the house. Ask anyone. Ask her bloody cleaner! The woman was a fussy old crone when it came to that rabbit hutch of a house.'

Hayes leapt up and stood eye to eye with him, judging the man's constraint to have been pushed to the limit.

'We haven't finished with you yet, Chambers. Sit down. You've answered none of my questions to my satisfaction and therefore we shall have to keep you here until you do.'

Bellamy tensed, watching the two face each other across the table. Suddenly, Maurice's temper cooled as quickly as it had erupted. They settled back in their seats.

'OK. What is it you want to know? Incidentally, my mother will vouch for the fact that I was home just after three that afternoon. She had come home from work early and realized as soon as I came in that I'd been on the booze. Sandy had bundled me out sharpish saying she was expecting someone and gave me the bottle to swig on the way home. I'd dumped it in the bottle bank but that didn't fool my lovely mamma. But that wasn't the worst of it: she guessed who I'd been drinking with. She hit the roof.'

'Because you'd deliberately broken the alcohol ban? You're hardly under age, Maurice. If you want to drink with a friend so what?'

He frowned. 'It's not that simple. You see she knew I'd been involved with Sandy over the car and supposed I'd fallen for her.'

'That you'd given Sandy money?'

'She had made enquiries – the used-car outfit had pasted its logo along the back window – and discovered the car had been paid for by someone matching my description, and thought Sandy and I were making out.'

'And were you?'

Maurice passed a trembling hand across his mouth, his concentration building up in the silence as he tried to frame the right words.

'Actually, no. Sandy was just a mate, like I said. But my mother didn't believe me and she has a siege mentality when it comes to family. But she can tell you I was at home for the rest of the day – in fact, she locked me in her study, which has enough security to double for a bank vault. I phoned Delphi to come home and sort it out but she was busy rehearsing in Oxford so I was left to stew till Dad got back.'

'You poor sod,' Bellamy breathed.

Hayes sent Maurice home in a squad car and Bellamy followed him to his office.

'That poor beggar banged up like a naughty kid. Can you believe it, sir?'

'As a matter of fact, I can't.'

Twenty-four

Briefing Supt Waller was never easy and explaining away the swift release of his chief suspect was no help. Where did they go from here?

'Maurice Chambers isn't off the hook, sir. If you listen to the tape he's only got his mother to back up his story that he was back home before it got dark.'

'Which doesn't constitute a watertight alibi, does it? Because what neither he or his mum knows yet is that the maggot expert, Professor – er – Glyn?, says the flies got to work in daylight, eh? Everyone assumed the killing was done after dark but with the inquest opening tomorrow we'll need all the back-up we can get. It will be adjourned, of course, while the investigation is on, but we don't want Scotland Yard called in, do we? Let's face it, everything stacked up against Chambers is circumstantial, there's no forensic evidence linking him with the crime, but once the press get on to the fact that it's an interesting case, the fat will be in the fire.'

'He admits being at the house that day and made no bones about his fingerprints being on the bottle and probably spattered all over the crime scene but, yes, we can't pin him down further than that.'

'Well, perhaps it's time we made a fresh start, Hayes. Got back to square one and saw the picture from a different angle. See what turns up. If this Prentice woman was a professional escort as well as a freelance hairdresser, her contacts must go into double figures and then some. I've set up an incident room in the Baptist chapel in the village and we've been offered some extra support staff.'

'I'll drive back to London after the inquest and see what else I can dig up. This friend of hers, the partner in the escort agency, hasn't been entirely free with information. There may be a way of leaning on Mrs Carberry, find out if she's been blacklisted at any of the big hotels.'

Waller stacked up the file and handed it back, dismissing Hayes with a curt wave of the hand.

The preliminary inquest was brief and with the total dearth of family or grieving friends the procedure seemed coldly businesslike. A full inquest was put on hold. Hayes spoke to Hardcastle, the solicitor, as they left the courtroom and they agreed that releasing the body for burial would tidy things up.

'I'll put an announcement in the local paper and send details of the funeral to Mrs Prentice's contacts at the nursing homes. That should draw in quite a gathering, wouldn't you say? An attractive woman like that must have had lots of friends.'

'Will the old lady, Mrs O'Brien, be instructing you?'

'I have spoken to her on the telephone. Naturally she is extremely upset. Mrs Prentice directed in her will that cremation would be her choice and Mrs O'Brien suggested I deal with the arrangements as I see fit. The poor woman has been hit badly by this tragedy, the manager of the home informs me, and is unlikely to be well enough to travel.'

Hayes left Bellamy and his team at the mercy of the Superintendent, who was hell bent on getting the lads on to a re-examination of the witness statements and off their backsides with more door-to-door enquiries in the village. Waller was a stickler for the old methods, having little respect for whiz kids crouched over computer terminals.

Hayes would be glad to get away, the atmosphere having nosedived since Waller had decided to step in.

He decided to postpone a visit to old Mrs O'Brien and instead to collar Jenny Robbins to accompany him to the detox clinic near Aylesbury where Maurice had been incarcerated after his release from prison. She took the wheel.

'I want you to get back to this girlfriend Chambers was making up to at Westlake House, the one who was free with the loose talk before. You established some sort of rapport with her, didn't you?'

'Hardly heart-to-heart, sir. I think she just liked having a girl of her own age to talk to. Most of the other patients looked pretty self-absorbed to me, not the sort to spend time with a kid who wanted someone to chat to that wasn't on the staff. Are you after more on Maurice?'

'Not unless it comes up. I'm more interested in any contact she may have had with Sandy Prentice. Did she know her? Had her hair cut for instance? And particularly did she know that Chambers was probably getting his leg over Sandy at the same time as sweet-talking her? Anything useful would be great – we're scraping the barrel here. On quite another tack, are you going to this concert at the weekend? The Florian Brandt recital?'

Jenny glanced across sharply, wondering if his interest in Pippa was greater than her housemate realized or whether her boss was truly keen to hear this boring tenor warble through a stack of German songs.

'Er, no. It's not really my bag. Pippa's rushed off her feet with this festival. You know how it is: last minute crises, people getting flu just at the wrong moment. Tickets are sold out, though, so it must be me.'

'Yeah, takes all sorts. Now listen, when we get to this place you follow me into the administrator's office and we'll play it straight this time, ask permission for you to interview this girl informally – keep it light, see. And while you're trotting round the grounds with Miss Whatsisname—'

'Mary Turner.'

'Right. Well, in the mean-time I'll try and impress the head man, a Dr Longley, with the seriousness of our investigation into every aspect of Sandy Prentice's work here. OK?'

They arrived at the impressive portico of Westlake House just as tea was being served, the enticing aroma of toasted muffins wafting through the hall as they waited for the receptionist to ring through.

Jenny Robbins tacked on to Hayes' heels, hearing the muffled laughter and clatter of teacups from some distant dining room like a rerun of her brief career in a psychiatric hospital. Not that Westlake House bore any resemblance to that state institution, but despite the bowls of fresh flowers and the deep pile rugs covering polished parquet there was an undeniable ambiance of confinement here, an impression of control.

Hayes and his red-haired sidekick were admitted to a panelled room where Dr Longley rose to greet them. They accepted cups of tea and seated themselves on sofas ranged about a low table. The administrator was a bearded fellow, strongly built and with the gleaming smile of a man well used to dealing with difficult situations.

Hayes launched into a summary of the case and after an initial retrenchment the doctor eventually agreed that Jenny could have a chat with Mary Turner if accompanied by Matron. Hayes quickly agreed and Dr Longley called his secretary to take Jenny to the dining room. He rang through to Matron explaining the situation and suggested the conversation with their patient be conducted privately in the sick bay.

When the women had left, Hayes reassured Longley that his officer would in no way disturb Mary Turner with a tactless interrogation. 'We are only trying to gain some insight into a possible romantic triangle between Mary, a young man who was being treated here and the dead woman.'

'Special friendships do spring up in our little community, of course. We try to defuse any serious involvements, especially among our young people, who are vulnerable and emotionally sensitive.'

'Tell me what you can about Sandra Prentice.'

The doctor leaned forward as if to put Hayes into clear focus.

'Well, one can't libel the dead so may I be frank, Chief Inspector? I personally was not entirely happy with this person. Mrs Prentice came with excellent references, of course, and worked here for almost three years. We were not her only employers, and specializing as she did in work at nursing homes and private clinics such as Westlake House, she was used to handling difficult people. Some of our guests here are under great strain. As voluntary patients we cannot press any treatment on them, of course, and, in fact, if he so wished any patient could just walk out of here, as indeed some do. But generally they arrive with good intentions and the enormity of the fees is an incentive to work at it.'

'Your success rate is good?'

'Middling. But, yes, on the whole, we are winning. That is why the self-esteem of each patient is vital and so our hairdresser, our manicurist and our personal trainers are as important as the medical staff.'

'You mentioned you were not entirely happy with Mrs Prentice's work here.'

Dr Longley puffed out his cheeks in a comically Gallic gesture. 'Her *work* was first class, no complaints there, and her friendly manner was cheering. Sad people need lots of encouragement and looking good is part of our therapy. Now, what I am going to say is unproven and I would not share my misgivings with you on any official basis. But rumours came to my hearing of unsuitable relationships developing with some of Mrs Prentice's regular clients.'

'Men?'

'Oh yes. Haircuts were not reserved for our ladies. Matron tipped me off that jealousies were festering in certain quarters and, as I said, our patients are frequently damaged people with huge struggles to overcome addictions of many sorts. A friendly squeeze of the hand can be misconstrued and as our residents are all wealthy people or those whose families are in a financial position to support their treatment here, tipping – which incidentally is frowned upon – can get out of hand, and quite substantial sums were passing which were a cause for concern.'

'You suspected services were extended beyond hair-dressing?'

'Quite possibly. But the real crisis came about when one of our mature gentlemen suddenly discharged himself after making an allegation that Mrs Prentice had stolen a valuable watch. He refused to call the police and frankly losses of personal property are often quickly resolved, our patients, because of their medication, often being forgetful. The nursing staff are used to recriminations of various kinds and on this occasion I accepted Mrs Prentice's denials in good faith.'

'But it happened again?'

'Regrettably so. Without evidence of any kind matters could not have been properly investigated but Mrs Prentice took umbrage and decided to leave. She continued to be employed in other establishments and I thought it wise to let the matter rest.'

'Did you have any personal opinion on her honesty?'

'Just a gut feeling that she had everything on her side and my poor patients, already stressed and lacking assert-iveness, had probably been hoodwinked in some way, had perhaps received intimacies that were later withdrawn, thus putting their complaints in a dubious and possibly embarrassing light.' The doctor shrugged. 'Not much to go on, Chief Inspector, but if it's background information you are building up perhaps you should bear in mind that all may not have been what it seemed with Sandra Prentice.'

Twenty-five

Pippa Cooper's phone call came out of the blue.

'Hi, stranger! Jenny tells me you're still working your balls off on this village stabbing. Time for a break, we decided – she gave me your mobile number, strictly off limits, I'm sure, but I said I had had an idea. How do you fancy a peep at Brandt's rehearsal followed by supper on my expenses? I was supposed to entertain the bloody man and his agent but my boss has elbowed his way in to do the honours himself.'

'Doesn't trust you with his star turn?'

'Something like that. Well, what do you say? An evening off will give your little grey cells no end of a boost and if you're as gummed up on this case as Jenny says, a rehearsal may be all you'll have time for.'

Hayes was in the throes of catching up on his paperwork, but the prospect of abandoning his desk for a night out seemed too good to miss.

'Well, thanks, Pippa. Sounds terrific. Where shall we meet?'

'I'm at the hall now. Florian's checking out the piano. Johnny's here, looking as boot-faced as an undertaker, but I'm hoping Brandt will buck the trend and say thumbs up on the instrument and the venue. My boss is on his tippy-toes being ever so accommodating.' She laughed. 'Come over when you can. I'll leave a message with the doorman to let you in and you'll find me at the back of the stalls with a bag of popcorn at the ready.'

Hayes slid into the darkened auditorium like a trout in a stagnant pool and squeezed Pippa's hand without a word.

On the floodlit stage Florian Brandt was in fierce conference with two older men, his hands pumping the air in emphasis.

'That's his agent and my boss, Mike Fitzwilliam,' Pippa whispered. 'I bet Florian's wanting to change the repertoire. Mike'll go bananas if he's forced to amend the programme.'

Hayes nodded, mesmerized by the drama on stage. Delphi sat at the piano, pale as a ghost, seemingly indifferent to the argument. It took several minutes before Brandt resumed his place, standing with one hand on the piano. Delphi tensed, her spine straight as an arrow as she perched on the edge of the bench and, after a nod from Brandt, started to play.

The voice soared in the empty auditorium, sending a shiver to Hayes' nerve ends. He gripped Pippa's hand, oblivious to her sharp glance before relaxing in her seat. His gaunt profile was etched against the dimness like a charcoal drawing and she recognized all too clearly that this odd bloke was cast from a different mould than the average copper. She had brought along her opera glasses and in between scribbling in a shorthand notebook kept a watchful eye on the proceedings through the binoculars.

At the end of the song cycle Delphi slumped at the piano, waiting for the inevitable conference to settle its differences. She seemed merely a spare part in this performance, her expertise rendering her invisible. Hayes longed to applaud but just grinned at Pippa, silently mouthing his approval as she rose to join the party on stage, passing him the binoculars with a wink.

Johnny Todd had joined the group, standing behind Delphi like a guardian angel. Hayes observed the animated free-for-all closely through the opera glasses, intrigued by the backstage view of a star performance. He waited, unseen in the back row, watching the interplay between the rump of the party. His interest shifted to Todd, who seemed, even from Hayes' oblique view, to be under considerable strain. And no wonder. Practically dropping a piano on the mother of his *protégée* was bad enough, but the backlash to his business of hiring concert grands to events such as the festival could be serious. There was also the possibility of being sued by Iris Chambers, or at the very least blackballed by this important member of local society.

Johnny looked all in, his hair dampening the neck of his sweatshirt with perspiration as he closed down the Bechstein, the barely noticeable limp Melanie Crabbe, the cleaner, had mentioned now causing him to lurch awkwardly as he rounded the piano to check the height of Delphi's bench. Hayes' binoculars idly swept over his target who wore black jeans and a grey top, his sub-fusc attire as unassuming as the man himself.

On a hunch, Hayes zoomed in on his feet and bolted upright. Maurice Chambers had been right: even the bloody piano tuner wore Lakeland boots. How was it he'd never noticed the popularity of these hiking boots before? Were they all the rage with the younger element in Oxford? The party broke up, Brandt and his agent swept to the wings by Pippa's boss.

Hayes dropped the binoculars in his lap and sat quietly watching the remaining trio on stage, recalling Jason's insistence that he had seen Maurice Chambers crossing the field later in the afternoon of Sandy's murder. Longish hair, he had said, and 'a man with a limp'. Blimey, maybe the silhouette Jason had caught sight of wasn't Chambers at all but Johnny Todd. He was as matey with the Prentice woman as Chambers, according to Melanie.

Hayes frowned, the possibility lapping around in his brain that Jason had got it wrong . . .

Finally, after brief congratulations all round, the three left on the platform started to pack up. Pippa helped Delphi collect her annotated sheet music and they held a subdued conversation which Hayes failed to hear from his seat in the darkness. Penny did not bring him forward, for which he was glad: Delphine Chambers was probably in no mood to socialize with the man who had been grilling her brother at the police station for most of the morning. He watched Pippa peck Johnny's cheek and hug Delphi before seeing them off. She shaded her eyes, squinting into the dark, and beckoned Hayes to follow her out through a side exit.

Later, settled in a bistro on the edge of the city, they relaxed over a bottle of Beaujolais and rehashed what had been for each of them a difficult day.

'Jenny said you've been trying to put together a profile of the poor Prentice woman. I wish I'd known her, she sounds fascinating.'

'Difficult to read. Everyone you talk to thought Sandy Prentice a nice friendly soul, but the worms are starting to come out of the woodwork.'

'Ouch! That was a horrible simile. There's a whisper going about the village about the discovery of the body. Maggots! Good God. It sounds like a horror movie.'

'Every murder's a horror movie. Even ordinary road accidents can give you nightmares, believe me, and don't even ask about suicides on the railway line.'

'Enough sad talk. Drink up and give me the low-down on this expensive detox clinic that all the pop stars and raddled models run to when they need flushing out.'

Hayes smiled. 'An expensive nuthouse, if you ask me. A cushioned retreat for all sorts, not just alcoholics and druggies. Frankly, I think half the patients just want to get off the world for a break. And, as it happens, I saw no soap stars or celebrities of any sort so the reputation as an all-star bolt-hole's probably just hype.'

'Bet you wouldn't know a soap star if she fell into your soup, Roger. Anyway, what goes on?'

'Oh, a lot of group therapy, guitar-playing, communing with trees, chanting serenity prayers, yoga, the usual clap-trap.'

'Well, it must work. I saw on the Internet that a private detox programme can cost thousands a week!'

'Well, I won't order another bottle then, shall I?'

Pippa slapped his hand. 'I told you. I'm paying tonight. Tell you what, why don't we press on back to your place and enjoy a few drinks and a take-away with home comforts?'

'Sounds a good idea to me.'

Next morning the whole evening seemed to blur in his memory into one continuous round of banter, finalizing in them both collapsing into Hayes' feather pillows like a pair of turtle doves. Altogether a night to remember.

Jenny Robbins' report lay on his desk but, frankly, there wasn't much in it. Mary Turner had clammed up in the presence of Matron and the informal girly talk Jenny had planned stiffened, Mary reduced to monosyllabic phrases barely audible to the increasingly irritable listeners. Eventually Matron stood up, closing down the interview.

'I think Mary's had enough, my dear. Isn't that right, Mary? You knew Sandy as a kind listener but she let you down, didn't she? Turned her charm on Maurice who, let's face it, basically prefers older women.'

The object of their interest sat on the edge of a bed in the san, looking for all the world like a waif. She was, as Jenny Robbins well knew, twenty-five years old, the skinny adolescent disguise a sad reflection of the age in which the unfortunate kid had chosen to maroon herself.

Jenny gave up, shook hands with Matron and impulsively clasped Mary's bony shoulders in a sisterly embrace.

Hayes stuffed Robbins' report in his file and bleakly watched grey clouds gather round a watery morning sun like muggers intent on GBH. He had to get out, get some perspective on this rotten case. His excuse would be an urgent need to interview Marie O'Brien, the frail old lady who probably knew Sandy better than anyone but who, following the shock of the brutal killing, was probably sinking fast and might, if he delayed much further, be beyond any questioning at all.

The phone rang. It was Bellamy calling from the Old Rectory where he had been dispatched first thing to check out the number of times Johnny Todd had recently been called to the house to service Delphi's pianos.

'Thought you ought to know, sir, that Maurice Chambers 'as gone missing. His father's here now in a right old state. Mrs Chambers is raising the roof, insists the police have hounded her son into a breakdown.'

'Disappeared, or just gone off after a row with Dad?'

'No, scarpered into the blue. Nobody knows where he's vanished to. Mr Chambers swears there was no showdown when the lad was brought back after questioning but it looks bad if he does anything stupid. Maurice isn't exactly stable is he, sir?'

Hayes tried to damp things down. 'Probably pushed off on a bender. He'll turn up when he's sober. Tell Mr Chambers we'll keep an eye open, Bellamy, and try to keep the lid on things at the house, we don't want the Super getting the idea we've frightened the horses. Get back here and sit on the phone. I'm off to London to check out a couple of things. Ring me if there are any developments.'

'Well, there is one other thing, sir. Mrs Chambers is discharging herself from hospital, her old man says. He's trying to set up a full time nurse to move in – apparently she flipped as soon as she heard the police were chasing her boy, insisted on going home. And worse, Noel Chambers' car's gone an' all. The doctors are not happy,' he concluded in that lugubrious tone Hayes knew all too well. Downplaying a situation was more than the sergeant could muster with any conviction.

Hayes replaced the receiver. 'Shit!'

Maurice on the loose with no licence and no car insurance was bad enough, having his mother on the rampage shooting off accusations of police harassment was the last thing he needed.

Twenty-six

Hayes drove straight to Sydenham to seek out old Mrs O'Brien. He arrived just after the residents had had their early lunch, quite the most inconvenient time, he was informed, because 'the elderly folk take an afternoon nap until two or sometimes even later'. The receptionist was adamant. 'You should have made an appointment, Inspector. Mrs O'Brien is not really up to visitors at the moment.'

He was still heatedly pressing his case as a senior nurse arrived to start her shift. The dragon at the gate called her over and described the policeman's determination to speak to the old lady.

The nurse eyed Hayes with distrust but, hearing out his appeal, finally relented, calling him into her office to the relief of the receptionist, who gladly washed her hands of the business and got back to her computer.

'My name's Angela Wooldridge and I am the sister in charge of Mrs O'Brien's unit. Please take a seat.'

Hayes introduced himself and launched into a summary of the Prentice case with special reference to Mrs O'Brien's dealings with Hardcastle, the solicitor.

She nodded. 'Yes, I see your point. As it happens I am all too familiar with the case. Let me explain. I also, like Sandy Prentice, have reason to be particularly fond of Auntie Marie, as we used to call her. I was one of Marie's many foster-children and knew Sandy at school. She was the girl next door.'

Hayes breathed deeply, hardly believing this astonishing bit of luck.

'You've known her all this time?'

'We lost contact when Sandy left home.'

'But she kept in touch with Mrs O'Brien.'

'Oh yes, and Marie shared the scraps of news from all her charges so I was always pretty well up to date. I continued to see Marie on a regular basis and Sandy called in from time to time. As I said, Sandy's parents lived next door. She was an only child and naturally was attracted to the rough and tumble in the neighbouring household. Marie had a series of foster children of all ages over the years and the atmosphere in our house, though chaotic, was always loving and easygoing. Sandy's mum and dad were strict Baptist and disapproved of the O'Brien set-up. At one point the social services people received a complaint about the number of kids Marie took in – her fostering was always by private arrangement and, to be honest, her heart was too big for her head. We suspected it was the Woods next door who had reported Marie to the authorities: several kids were taken away to children's homes, leaving just me and the Zeto twins who it was agreed Marie could cope with. She was a wonderful mother to all of us and the Christmas cards from her grown-up "babies" as she called them, pile up like a snowdrift each year.'

The woman stared out of the window, lost in a reverie of happier times.

'Mrs Prentice was clearly very fond of her to leave everything to someone who wasn't even a relative.'

'Yes. But we all loved her. Marie's very frail these days because of her arthritis but her mind's as sharp as a tack, she can give you the names and birthdays of all her old charges.'

'But your path never crossed Sandy's after she left home?'

'Only recently when she insisted Marie must move into a nursing home. The poor dear was ever so reluctant to lose her independence but eventually Marie agreed if she could come here, knowing I was on hand. I sometimes met Sandy on her brief visits here but she was always in a terrible rush and, to be truthful, we didn't have much in common apart from our affection for Marie.'

'This place is expensive, I take it.'

'Oh very. It was extremely generous of Sandy to put up the money herself, wasn't it? Mind you, her own parents passed away years ago I've been told so maybe she hadn't anyone left to care for. And Marie has settled here wonderfully well.'

'I would like to speak with her if I may. I need every bit of background information I can muster – there are gaps, personal details, the name of a man-friend who Sandy confided to her business partner was very special. You heard nothing of this?'

Angela Wooldridge shook her head, her iron grey hair cut in a severe bob, her sturdy frame impressive as she rose to shake his hand.

'You must excuse me, Chief Inspector, duty calls. But if you promise to keep your visit brief Marie may be able to tell you a little more.'

She led him upstairs and along a brightly painted corridor, and tapped on an oak door.

'Marie sleeps very little,' she whispered. 'Says catnaps only ruin a good night's rest.'

Hayes nodded, nervously adjusting his tie, wondering if chasing up an old woman in a retirement home was really the best use of his time. Sister Wooldridge showed him in, her cheerful 'Hello there' rousing a white haired lady who despite her stated disapproval of a siesta had clearly been enjoying a nice little snooze. After introducing him Wooldridge left them to it, Hayes drawing up a chair close to Mrs O'Brien and hoping against hope that the assurances about her total recall were true.

Marie O'Brien carried her years with grace, her bird-like figure almost lost in a large armchair heaped about with cushions. She wore a blue paisley-patterned dress which matched almost exactly the forget-me-not eyes. Her feet were propped on a low stool, her crippled hands lying in her lap like clenched fists, the arthritic joints painful to witness. Her voice had a soft Irish lilt and she smiled encouragement at the young man sitting on the edge of his chair, his discomfiture in her lavender scented room all too apparent.

'Do make yourself easy, my dear. I've been expecting you.'

Hayes stiffened. 'Really?'

'Oh indeed I have. Someone was bound to get around to me eventually. I want to help all I can. My poor Sandy. How could something so bad happen to such a lovely girl?'

'You have known her for many years, Sister Wooldridge tells me.'

'Oh yes. A very quiet child at first but she managed to slip over to our side of the fence as often as she could. Loved being with all the other children, of course, and as her mum and dad were both working it was easy for our little Sandy to join in the fun and games for an hour or two after school.'

'They disapproved?'

'Very strict religious folk and very good people at heart, but our house was a honeypot Sandy just couldn't resist. At home it was all homework and piano practice; the Woods had high hopes for their daughter.

'The fostering started by chance. My husband worked on the Underground, awkward shifts and not much in the way of wages, so when a widowed neighbour died in a road accident and the relatives asked us to take her boy in, it seemed like Fate. We had no children of our own, Reg and me, and Charlie Bennett was the first of many. Angela who brought you up here was one of my long-stay girls but in those days the rules were looser and people like me who had private arrangements were left more or less on our own.'

'But later the authorities clamped down, took some of your foster children into care, I believe.'

'Overcrowding, they said. Tragic. One or two never settled after that . . .' Her voice trailed away and Hayes paused, seeing the tears gather. But she rallied and blew her nose, and he drew her back to his quest for the real Sandy Prentice.

'I have spoken to Mr Hardcastle, your solicitor, and without divulging any details he informs me you are the sole beneficiary.'

She nodded. 'Silly, isn't it? An old fool like me. But Sandy insisted and when I had thought about it I persuaded her to let me make a will too. It started as a bit of a joke between us because no sane person would assume I would outlive my darling girl now, would they? But Sandy was always good for a laugh and she knew, underneath, I needed to put my name to an injustice which has haunted me all these years. You see, one of my little boys who was taken away by the social people needed all my love and care. I should never have let them take him away. It is a bitter regret. They said he needed much more hospital treatment and as by then my poor Reg had passed away and my arthritis was getting really bad they put it to me it would be better for Tim if he was where there were staff to supervise his treatment.'

'The boy had mental problems?'

She frowned. 'Oh no, nothing like that. Our Tiny Tim as we called him – from that Dickens book, you know – was as bright as a button. Small for his age and, like they said, in and out of hospital for years. His mother was very young. She asked me to take care of him so she could get a job and for a while she did send money each week but then she stopped writing and never came to see her little boy after she moved away – she left no forwarding address. I could understand her problem, she just couldn't cope. But Tim needed her and she left him on my doorstep like a bundle of dirty washing, poor child. My Reg got mad, threatened to report her to the police but I said no, Tim's fine with us, the money's not so important and I expect she will turn up when she can afford it. But when he got to six and a half I let him down too, just like his mum, and those social busybodies put him in a home.'

The old lady dabbed at her cheeks with a handkerchief clutched in her claw-like hand.

'Did the boy have no father?'

She gathered herself to answer.

'Well, yes, in a way. We had the mother's former address in Norfolk, which was that of her husband, a farmer, a Mr Carter, but when my Reg wrote and told him what had happened he phoned us back and explained about the divorce. It seems Timmy was not his child, illegitimate, he said, and what with the poor boy's constant hospital stays he said he hardly knew him. She was pregnant when she left Norfolk and later, after the divorce was final, she told Mr Carter she was getting married again and moving abroad. He asked her about Timmy but she said he had died on the operating table. Such a wicked lie! To add salt to the wound she told him the new baby wasn't his either, which he said wasn't much of a surprise, his wife being the flighty sort who had caused gossip in the village. The split was bitter, you could tell, but when my Reg said we still had his stepson who was a lovely little boy, he didn't want to know, said he'd washed his hands of her and her kids. So now you can see, Inspector, I was so sad for my poor Timmy who had been dumped on us and then dumped by me into a so-called "Home". He was badly treated there so I found out years later. It made my heart bleed when I read about it in the papers – some nasty housemaster was brought to court over it, had assaulted several of the young boys in his care. I wrote to the authorities asking if I could have Timmy back but they said he had been "rehabilitated", whatever that means.'

'Adopted by a family?'

'Oh no. He was quite a big lad by then and had done well at school. They put him into one of those state boarding schools and said he was exceptionally gifted. That made me feel a bit better. While he was away at school, I would sometimes send him postcards asking how he was getting on but he never wrote back and once he left I had no address so I never got round to telling him how sorry I was.'

'I take it this is the young man you've named in your will?'

'Sandy understood how I felt. She helped me arrange all the legal twaddle with her lawyer and at the time I felt she was only humouring an old lady. I had no money of my own to speak of – making a will was just my silly way of putting my mind at rest, squaring my conscience about Tiny Tim.'

'Not so tiny now, I imagine.'

'I haven't seen him since the day they took him away to that horrible home, but Sandy sought him out for me through a detective agency and got to know him well, spoke very highly of my favourite boy. So there you go, Inspector, even a sad story like Sandy's will have a happy ending after I've gone.'

'The lad knows he's been named? With all the publicity about Mrs Prentice's death surely he will be visiting you?'

'I told Sandy not to bother the boy with me – it's too late to be doing with an old woman and I didn't want him to feel badgered. After all it was just my little gesture, it's not as if my small savings would change his life, it just made me easy to feel I had done something at long last.'

'But things have changed, haven't they?'

'Mr Hardcastle has tried to explain everything but I can't take it in. This murder has broken my spirit, I feel as if this wicked world has taken my soul. What have I, an old woman, to live for if a lovely girl like my Sandy can be snatched away by a madman?'

There was a knock on the door. Angela Wooldridge entered, eyeing Hayes with a severe glance as she noted the old lady's distress.

'Time to go, Chief Inspector.'

Hayes rose, raising a hand in mute appeal.

'Just one more question, Mrs O'Brien. Did Sandy mention the name of her fiancé? An impending marriage?'

Marie O'Brien shook her head and stared back, as confused as if he had proposed himself as a possible suitor.

'No, never. Sandy never spoke of any engagement. You've got it all wrong, dear. She would have told me.'

Hayes sighed, leaning across to touch her knotted fingers. 'You're right. Just a hunch. I hope I haven't upset you too much, asking all these questions.'

She smiled and waved him away, exhausted by her visitor yet strangely at peace, the raw edge of guilt a little smoother for sharing her regrets with a stranger. He turned away and followed the sister back to Reception.

'I hope your little chat helped with your investigation.'

'Not much, I'm afraid. The old lady was rather obsessed with another old story. About one of her charges,Tiny Tim. You may remember him yourself perhaps.'

They stood under the porch, sheltering from the heavy drops of rain that seemed to be shaping up as a prelude to a real downpour.

She laughed. 'Old people get fixed on something and can't let it go: sorry you were sidetracked by that old chestnut. A poor wee scrap he looked from the photos in Marie's album. Tiny Tim wasn't his real name, of course. I only found out his proper name when the solicitor sent copies of the will for her to sign. She needed a witness and I asked the director to do the honours. I'm one of the executors, you see.'

'She left you nothing? Everything to this waif?'

'So what? At the time it seemed just a little fancy to salve her conscience about choosing me and the Zito twins to stay and allowing Tim and the other two children to be taken away. Sandy understood this and it wasn't as if Marie had enough in the bank to squabble over. None of us could ever guess that Marie would outlive Sandy, could we? Marie's will was a means of dying peacefully, knowing she had done her best to put it right – me having been one of the lucky ones who was chosen to stay put me right out of the picture. Tim was the one who suffered.'

'As a matter of interest, what is his name?'

'John Wesley Todd.'

Twenty-seven

Hayes drove to the nearest layby and smoked several cigarettes. Where to from here? John Wesley Todd. Of all the crazy coincidences! It turned the whole case on its head.

He phoned Bellamy. 'Any developments?'

'No, sir. Chambers is still missing.'

'Forget bloody Chambers. Did you check at the house and find out how many times the piano tuner's been in during the past few months?'

'The piano tuner? Oh, you mean Todd. Well, I asked the girl and she got quite stroppy. But she eventually agreed to look in her diary and there's no mileage there, sir. The Chambers girl's got no time for the bloke, if that's what you're looking for. Todd's been coming in to tune the upright in the studio pretty often because the room's damp and she keeps calling him back to give it another going-over.'

'How often?'

'About four times this year – not over the top for a fussy madam like Miss Chambers, but the arrangement's dead professional, no hanky panky there. In fact, I got the feeling she was pretty fed up with Johnny Todd, and not just because of her mother's accident. She said he was "too controlling" but wouldn't say any more.'

Hayes sighed. 'OK. Just a thought. I'll be back about five. Tell the Super I'm on to a new lead and need to see him urgently, tonight if possible.'

The silence at the other end spoke volumes, Bellamy forecasting a swift falling-out between Waller and his new chief inspector. Hayes hadn't got a clue how to handle the boss. Waller liked to steer his own way and Hayes' detours up God knew how many dead ends only reduced the murder investigation to Blind Man's Buff.

'Right you are, sir. I'll see what I can do.'

When he got back to the village Waller was pacing the incident room in his shirtsleeves, his fleshy jowls flushed with irritation. The rump of the murder squad not already running round Newton Greys chasing increasingly nebulous leads sat disconsolately like kids kept in after school, looking in their bleary-eyed acceptance of Waller's ranting like a bunch of punch-drunk boxers.

They looked up expectantly as Hayes breezed in, revived in the expectation of a fresh target in the Superintendent's sights.

'You follow me, my lad,' Waller barked and strode into a back room, leaving Hayes to close the door on the eager-eyed team in the outer office.

Waller slumped at a table, glaring at Hayes almost with loathing.

He seated himself as far away as possible, crossed his legs and smiled apologetically.

'You were quite right, sir,' he said earnestly. 'I was barking up the wrong tree chasing Morry Chambers. I took your advice and went off to interview Sandy Prentice's old lady, the one she's left all her money to.'

'Is this relevant? Because I'm in no mood for any more of your fandangoes, Hayes.'

'Bear with me, sir.' He outlined his conversation with Hardcastle about the will and went on to explain Mrs O'Brien's relationship with the dead woman.

'All very touching, I'm sure, but where's all this leading to?'

'One of the old woman's foster children – she had looked after a whole bundle of kids over the years – well, one of the long stayers is now a sister at the nursing home where Sandy Prentice chose to retire Mrs O'Brien. Sister Wooldridge knew Prentice from way back and reckoned if there were any secrets about our corpse Mrs O'Brien would be in on it. But the thing I was after, the name of the chap Prentice told her agency partner was to be husband number two, drew a blank. Either Prentice made up the story to impress Mrs Carberry or it was information too hot to share even with Mrs O'Brien. Especially Mrs O'Brien, if my hunch pays off.'

'Get on with it, man!'

'The will's the key, sir. Prentice left everything to Mrs O'Brien and the old lady made a will almost simultaneously leaving all her worldly goods to guess who? Johnny Todd.'

'The piano tuner? Why?'

'Sod's law the bloody piano tuner turns out to have been another one of her foster children.'

'And Prentice knew him as a kid?'

'No. He left the O'Brien set-up when he was six years old. Sandy would have been out at work by then and even if she did hear about Tiny Tim, as they called him, the poor little tyke was in and out of hospital most of the time having surgery on a deformed foot.'

Waller's florid complexion had visibly paled.

'You think the piano tuner was shaping up to marry Prentice?'

'Well, she did like younger men.'

'What about young Chambers?'

Hayes shrugged. 'Possible, but he'd be a bit of a wild card even for Sandy Prentice: an ex-con, an alcoholic and possible drug user dependent on his father's approval to keep his job in the family business? And from what I hear

Noel Chambers favours his daughter and would need little excuse to dump Maurice. Sandy must have worked it out that shackling herself to Maurice would only be a permanent drain on her own bank balance.'

'Morry's not exactly Best Boy with Dad since he got out of the Scrubs, I bet.'

'He's not his natural son, of course, though Noel Chambers brought him up with no expense spared, posh boarding school, a seat on the board, you can't say he hasn't done his best for the boy. Must be doing his nut waiting for the prodigal son to get arrested on another hit for drink driving.'

'Blood's thicker than water,' Waller observed darkly. He got up and went to a side cabinet. 'Fancy a thimbleful of malt, Hayes, just to keep the wheels oiled?'

Hayes blinked and mutely agreed, finding the volte face as alarming as the bollocking he had expected. They settled back to review the case against Todd.

Waller looked pensive. 'I don't buy it, Hayes. But it sounds more feasible than that cock-and-bull story you were trying to cobble together against young Chambers.'

'Well, Todd got to know Prentice reasonably well after she'd traced him through a private investigator, and he was in and out of her place in the village more often than an amateur pianist would need if the cleaner's story can be credited. The question is, did she admit to Todd that at the request of the old lady she had paid to track him down? And did she tell him about her own will and her close contact with his foster mother, Mrs O'Brien?'

'Why not? If they were such good pals why keep it a secret?'

'But suppose she tells Todd about her support of the old lady just to soften his attitude to her? An overgenerous gesture like paying thousands of pounds to cushion the final days of someone she didn't know all that closely.'

'But why would she want to impress a gimpy piano tuner?'

'Maybe she fancied him. For all we know Todd's a raging stud.'

'But supposing Todd harboured a grudge against the old woman for chucking him out as a kid and shoving him into care? These psychological buggers place big bucks on a long-standing grievance, the sort to sour the rest of the boy's life. Prentice shoving Mrs O'Brien in his face wouldn't earn any Brownie points, would it?'

'Frankly, I don't see it like that. I think Prentice wanted to settle down, move to the country with a sexy young bloke and enjoy her hard-earned cash with a nice hard-working guy with no vices. She was pretty loaded for a woman who pretended she was just a hairdresser. I doubt even the old woman knew about her career in the escort business. You should have seen that flat in Paddington, sir: nothing like the house in Didcot Drive, believe me.'

Waller frowned. 'Why did she move here, do you think? To be near Todd?'

'Why else? She was a good looking woman by all accounts and well caked up at the bank but Sandy Prentice was getting past her sell-by date. Her days with the Valentine Escorts were numbered and there wasn't room for two madams to run the business. Hairdressing's pretty routine even on the ritzy circuit Prentice commanded. Todd may not look much of a catch but, from her point of view, why not?'

Hayes outlined his findings about the footprints at the crime scene that might well match up with Todd's hiking boots. 'I shall have to have another go at Jason, see if he'd reconsider his identification of the limping man crossing the back field who he says was Chambers.'

'But Chambers doesn't deny crossing the bloody field on

his way home, does he? And why would Todd tramp about? He's got a perfectly decent car, I presume?'

'Well, he didn't park his van outside her house that afternoon, did he? We've been over and over the neighbours' statements and the van was well known, it's even got his name painted on it, and was seen often enough when he was allegedly tinkering with her baby grand.'

'You want to pull him in?'

'Yes.'

'I may be a stickler for the small print, Hayes, but it's only a couple of days ago you had to let Chambers go. I don't want another cock-up. The press are looking for a brick to heave at us as it is – weeks gone by since the woman was found and two bum arrests would give them a field day.'

Hayes rubbed his eyes, weary to death of the improbabilities in a case which was as full of holes as a smelly gruyère.

'Todd's the only one with a motive, sir. If he knew about the eighty-four-year-old's will in his favour and that Sandy Prentice was leaving everything to O'Brien, he only had to dispose of her and then bide his time to pick up the lot when the old woman croaked. Easier than marrying Prentice and having to kow-tow to an older woman for the next forty years.'

'My gut feeling goes right against this theory of yours that Prentice wanted to marry the bloke. Say, for instance, she confided in him that she was already engaged to someone else? If he knew about the two wills then Prentice getting wed would bugger up the sequence of inheritance, wouldn't it? He'd still cop for the old lady's little nest-egg but the big bucks would melt away if Prentice married someone else.'

'But there's no other man in the picture, sir. She would have told Mrs O'Brien if she had news like that. Telling Mrs Carberry that she planned to fix herself up with a nice rich husband was just panic talking. My money's on the piano tuner,' he insisted.

'OK, let's give it a shot,' Waller said at last, draining his whisky with the air of a man who had run out of options.

Twenty-eight

They got Johnny Todd out of bed before daylight and whisked him to the station before the press got wind of another suspect being brought in for questioning.

Hayes told Bellamy to get Todd some breakfast before shunting him into the interview room but he politely declined, his demeanour extraordinarily composed for a man dragged in on a murder inquiry.

They sat under a harsh light in the windowless room and Bellamy ran through the initial procedure like a dose of salts. Hayes craved a cigarette but put the urge to light up aside, guessing that his non-smoking suspect would view this unhealthy habit as a weakness.

'Right, let's get started. Now, Johnny, tell me when you last saw Sandy Prentice.'

Johnny Todd frowned, then silently took a diary from his back pocket and flipped through the pages.

'She wanted to book me in to see to her little Steinway on the fourth of October. But I told her my van was being serviced that day and I couldn't make it.'

'Which garage?'

'Proffitts on the Cowley Road. You can check. I hired a car but I can't work without my van, all my tools are there, and anyway I wanted a free day to work at home on Delphi's bookings.'

'You're her agent?'

'Not officially. But I use my contacts to get her work.

It's hard getting a toehold on the concert scene without at least some important awards to back you up.'

'And Delphi's not that good?'

He demurred. 'Not good enough as a solo artist, but I was trying to interest her in working with a friend of mine, a flautist. Two pretty girls with a decent repertoire can edge into the market sideways and Delphi needed all the experience she could get.'

'Are you in love with Delphine Chambers?'

Anger flickered across the dark face but his answer was controlled.

'I like to watch out for the girl, that's all.'

'Out of your class, you reckon?'

Todd's smile was bitter. 'That's a very old fashioned notion these days, Chief Inspector Hayes. Class? Status? You sound just like her mother.'

'But if you had money of your own, a substantial inheritance, say, you might be able to swing it, eh? Bring an inexperienced girl with ambitions beyond her ability round to your way of thinking, persuade her that you could push her up the ladder if she accepted you both professionally and romantically?'

Todd laughed. 'You make me sound like some sort of Svengali, Hayes. Really, Delphi is not interested in me as a boyfriend.'

'Have you asked her?' Bellamy cut in harshly.

Todd's eyes rested on the sergeant with distaste.

'Is the analysis of my relationship with Miss Chambers the sole object of this interview?'

'No, it's not,' Hayes retorted. 'Let's get back to the afternoon of the fourth of October, shall we? You refused to go to Didcot Drive that day?'

'At first. But Sandy insisted. Said she had a bottle of champagne on ice for us, had something important to tell me and wanted to celebrate.'

'Not a business call-out after all then?'

'As it turned out, no. I reluctantly agreed to drive over later in the afternoon but told her I had to be back in Oxford by six to pick up my van so I wouldn't be drinking.'

'What was Sandy Prentice celebrating?'

He lowered his eyes, noisily cracking his knuckles, a nervous gesture Hayes found extremely irritating. The silence lengthened.

'Come on now,' Bellamy barked, 'what did she want to see you for?'

'A private matter.'

'You refuse to comment?'

'It has absolutely nothing to do with your inquiry. It concerned a mutual friend.'

'Mrs O'Brien, your foster mother?'

His head shot up, the composure shattered.

'You dug out all that old history? Christ, man, I was only six when I left the O'Brien house! Give me a break.'

'But it's not such old history, is it?'

'As far as I'm concerned it is. Sandy should have kept her nose out of my private life. I had a rotten childhood if you want to know, and being pulled back to relive old miseries was of no interest to me.'

'Oh, wasn't it? What about the old lady's will?'

He laughed. 'Nickels and dimes. She may be a nice enough old bird but I can hardly remember her, to be honest. Sandy told me Mrs O'Brien felt bad about sending me away, chucking me in the bin with the other kids at the home, and felt guilty about what happened there, which was certainly not her fault. She asked Sandy to look me up, which is why she'd contacted the private eye. He turned up a whole lot of shit which I didn't want to know. Mrs O'Brien leaving her bits of savings to me in her will made her feel good but I didn't want to get involved and told Sandy so. She was paying the nursing home, you know; the old lady hasn't any crock of gold so forget it. Sandy had no business putting that agent on my tail and in the end she was using stuff for her own purposes.'

'What stuff?'

Todd turned mulish, shaking his head in silent obduracy.

'Did she tell you about her own will?'

'Blimey, Hayes! You got a bee in your bonnet? Sandy wasn't the sort to make any will – she thought she'd live for ever.'

'You're wrong. She did register a will. Left everything to Mrs O'Brien.'

'Nice touch.'

'She didn't mention it?'

'No. Why should she? I wasn't much interested in the old lady to be truthful. If you must know our bust-up was about something else entirely.'

'You turned down her offer.'

'What bloody offer?'

'Mrs Prentice moved down here to be near you?' Bellamy quietly proposed.

'No way. Why me? Are you suggesting she had designs on me, sergeant? That's stupid. Sandy Prentice had her own reasons for moving out of London and I was merely a footnote in her scheme of things.'

Hayes tried again to get his suspect to elaborate on the fatal afternoon.

'You do understand, don't you? The woman died the day you saw her. You were, as far as we can discover, the last person to see Sandy Prentice alive. Can we cut the crap, Todd? Did she have more to say than to tell you about Mrs O'Brien which, according to the old lady, she had asked Prentice to keep to herself? We can stay here all day and all night if you like. You're not seeing daylight till we get to the bottom of this.'

Johnny Todd sipped from a tumbler of water and, after another interminable silence, came to a decision.

'OK. Let's get this over with. Sandy insisted I call in and after I'd finished my work at home I drove over in the hired Fiat and parked on the main road. A delivery lorry was moving furniture into the house opposite and I didn't want to get boxed in that bloody cul-de-sac. I got there about three or just after. Sandy was pretty boozed, that was clear. She said she had shared the champagne with another friend as I was being so prissy about drink driving. I decided I'd give her ten minutes and then beat it.'

He glanced at Bellamy, whose lips were pursed in the effort to keep quiet.

'Yes, sergeant, you've guessed it. We had a blazing row. Sandy was in a filthy mood. Her boyfriend had backed off but she said she'd got information which would force his hand.'

'Second thoughts?' Bellamy retorted.

'Shut up, Bellamy. Let the man get a word in.'

Johnny Todd grinned, a nice smile Hayes noticed. In fact, when he thought about it, he wasn't at all a bad looking bloke. Curly dark hair, hazel eyes, small stature but years of heaving pianos about had given him the highly developed pecs of a weightlifter. He glanced at the neat feet shod in the ubiquitous hiking boots.

'What did you quarrel about?'

'She'd set her sights on this guy but it was the same old story: he couldn't see a way clear without losing out financially.'

'A businessman?'

'Yeah, sort of.'

'Local?'

'You guessed it. She moved to the village to put the screws on the poor devil but there was this difficulty of holding on to his job apparently. That was where I came in, she said.'

'How so?'

Todd narrowed his gaze, focusing intently on Hayes.

'You didn't know Sandy. She wasn't all sweetness and light like some thought. Sandy had a mean streak. She'd made it on her own but used methods that weren't always decent. She winkled out secrets from her clients and used them to get control. They were a vulnerable lot. It generally worked, and if it didn't she could turn very nasty. Sandy told me to back her up in a rotten scam and I refused.'

'She held a secret of yours?'

'Like a pistol to my head. Nothing criminal, I assure you, just a winch to drag this boyfriend of hers out in the open. I wasn't having any part of it and we were at each other's throats for nearly half an hour. I made to go and she didn't try to stop me but Sandy knew she could use me in this nasty business whether I agreed or not.'

'Blackmail?'

'Not really. A deal. A threat the weak link in this scenario would find it hard to walk away from.'

'A way of forcing her lover to jump? Well, we had better hear what it was, Todd, or we're likely to be at loggerheads till kingdom come.'

Todd refused to respond and, in a fit of desperation, Bellamy's voice rose, filling the stark room with undisguised rancour.

'Well, who was this poor sap you and Sandy Prentice were hounding? Let's stop playing games, Todd. It's got to be Chambers, hasn't it?'

The figure sitting at the other side of the table slumped as if his blood was seeping away.

'Yeah, OK. It was Chambers. Sandy thought he was going to marry her.'

'Morry Chambers?' Hayes croaked.

Todd straightened, grinning like a gargoyle.

'No, for pity's sake. Not Maurice. Noel. Noel was the target.'

Twenty-nine

Waller was in a good mood. He sat behind his empty desk like a gambler on a lucky streak, his cheeks glossy from his morning shave, the air faintly redolent of hair gel, his latest stab at getting in tune with the establishment smart set.

Hayes slipped into the room with the look of a worried man, an untidy bundle of papers tucked under one arm.

'Right. Sit down, Hayes, and let's get this fucking mess in some sort of order. Bellamy got a search warrant for Todd's place like I told him to?'

'Yes, sir. I said I'd run over to Oxford straight away.'

Waller nodded, stabbing out his cigarette, his eyes like gimlets. 'Well, get on with it, man. What did the Todd interview turn up?'

'He admits to being with Prentice on the fatal afternoon and says he left by three thirty but he hasn't any corroboration. Maurice Chambers was there before that and shared some champagne with the victim but she threw him out after a while and he took the bottle and finished it off on the way to the village recycling bin. Then he walked home.'

'Which fits in with your informant's statement that young Chambers was seen in the vicinity about that time?'

'Yes, sir. Jason is sticking to his identification and Chambers doesn't deny it. Says his mum will verify he was at home for the rest of the day, which leaves Todd as the last on the scene so far.'

'Do you think he did it?'

'He says he knew nothing about Sandy Prentice's will until we told him today, which was the thing on which we were basing our motive. If he was ignorant of the estate passing from Prentice to O'Brien and ultimately to himself we're looking for a different motive.'

'But he'd be a fool not to lie about it, wouldn't he? And he was clearly on a closer footing with Prentice than just being the bloody piano tuner. When did he first meet the woman?'

'She put a detective agency on his trail at the request of Mrs O'Brien, but Todd let slip that the PI found out more than just his current whereabouts. From what he said in the interview room, he and Prentice fell out about this information and her efforts to involve him in some sort of scam. There's no record of any payment by her to any detective agency but we're working on it.'

'But he admits to rowing with the woman the afternoon she died?' Waller persisted.

'Yeah. But he's keeping something back. Todd's not come clean on a number of issues. Perhaps when he's cooled off in a cell overnight he'll feel more co-operative.'

Waller lit another cigarette and pushed the pack over the desk to Hayes, who shook his head, vainly trying to present in a more positive light what was in anyone's book a rocky prosecution case.

'One surprise came out of it though, sir. Todd was in on the secret of Prentice's lover.'

'Chambers.'

Hayes laughed. 'Yeah, but Dad, not Morry. Todd says Noel Chambers was the Romeo.'

Waller's beady eyes widened in disbelief.

'Noel Chambers? Come off it, Hayes. You don't buy that one, do you?'

'It makes sense. Noel's the one with the money, and why

should Todd lie? I reckon Dad gave Morry the cash to buy his girlfriend a nice little motor and make sure she wasn't blown away by any dealers' talk. On Morry's side, having a lever on his father assured him of his place on the board of the family firm.'

'Does Maurice admit to this?'

'Not yet he doesn't, he's still missing. But I think we could twist his arm.'

'Noel Chambers, eh? Changes the scenery a bit, Hayes. You going public on this? Dodgy ground, lad, especially on the say-so of a nobody like Todd. We've no proof and Morry's not going to cough and put his dad on the spot. You reckon nobody knew about this so-called affair with Prentice? Not even her old dear?'

'Certainly not Mrs O'Brien. Todd seems to have been the only one in on it. And my guess is Sandy Prentice didn't share her secret for nothing. Todd hinted she wanted to get him in on some scam but he refused.'

'Blackmail?'

'Not strictly blackmail but possibly a back-up to let Noel know that the cat was out of the bag, that she was tired of waiting for him to leave his wife and was ready to tell Iris. It could have been something she'd been trying to force Todd to do for weeks, not this new scam he wouldn't talk about. But that's just my guess.'

'She moved to Newton Greys to be near Chambers?'

'Got tired of being his bit on the side.'

'She paid for the house with her own money?'

'Oh yes. She wasn't short in that department. The escort agency, Valentine's, paid handsomely and she may also have siphoned off cash from her rich clients as bumper hairdressing tips. The Aylesbury clinic was suspicious of her relations with one or two of their patients, and I wouldn't mind betting the Inland Revenue would be hard pressed assessing her taxable income bearing in mind her hairdressing and the escort lark were mostly cash arrangements and, at a guess, big handouts were regularly topping up her agency fees as well. Mrs Carberry says she was a popular date, had a sympathetic way with the punters. And if Chambers was buying her a car and giving her shares in his business, he probably lobbed out other expensive extras – the affair must have been going on for years, two at the very least.'

'Do we know how she met him?'

'Not yet. Might have been at the clinic when he was visiting Maurice, but my guess is he was introduced through the escort agency, a nice little frolic after one of his trade conferences. Mrs Carberry says clients are rarely known by their real names and if her partner was on to a good thing she would be the last to put his name on the line even if she knew it.'

'Prentice didn't confide in this Carberry woman?'

Hayes shrugged. 'Says not. Also we have no proof linking the mystery guy with Chambers. If it was Noel, he was bloody careful to keep himself off the record.'

Waller drew on his cigarette, eyeing Hayes with malevolent intensity.

'Ever thought you're barking up the wrong tree again, Hayes? Supposing – as we've more or less established – Morry Chambers came and went like he says on that afternoon, swiftly followed up by Todd, who may or may not have stayed only half an hour. What if Todd left like he said but a third man was watching? Hidden at the back, say? On a wet afternoon, coming on for dusk, the conservatory where she seems to have done her entertaining would have been lit up, wouldn't it? Quite a sideshow for a middle-aged jock who was getting the pinch from a lady who was cheek to cheek with two younger blokes in the space of a couple of hours? What if Chambers was waiting to jump Prentice when Todd gives him the signal?'

'You mean Noel was getting fed up with being forced

along by Prentice, knew that a divorce would entail a horrendously expensive wrangle over the business which Mrs Chambers had all but cornered for herself and—'

'Now do you see what I'm getting at? If Todd had already confronted him with the info that he knows about his affair and tried to put the boot in, Noel, no fool I assure you, despite his reputation for letting his old woman do all the donkey work at the garages, turns round and puts it to Todd that he'd do better changing sides?'

'The two of them to gang up on Prentice, you mean?'

'Easier to kill a fit woman if there are two of you in on it. Could be Todd's leading us up the garden path on this, Hayes. If Chambers decided the only way to finish the affair without Prentice pulling the house about his ears was to dispose of her once and for all, he'd be better off with a bit of muscle like Todd on his side, wouldn't he?'

Hayes bit his lip, trying to burst Waller's speculative balloon without a big bang.

'An interesting point, sir. But surely, by bringing Todd in on the murder Chambers would be laying himself open to a lifetime of blackmail?'

'Possibly. But we don't know much about Johnny Todd, do we? You reckon he's sweet on the daughter. With a bit of cash and the support of her dad, Todd could look a lot better in her eyes, eh? Tit for tat. A collusive couple of bastards both getting their own way and the only obstacle this pushy hairdresser-cum-part-time prostitute.'

'Whoa there, sir. That's taking a lot on guesswork and there's not a scrap of evidence linking Noel Chambers to the murder. Plenty of Todd's fingerprints about the place, and Morry Chambers' too come to that, but no bloodstained clothing, no weapon, no sighting of Noel lurking in the vicinity. We don't even know if he was at work that day or laying in an alibi with half a dozen worthy citizens at the golf club. And anyway, Chambers loves his daughter; seeing Todd as a son-in-law doesn't sound right to me.'

'Well, perhaps putting Noel on the scene is a step too far,' Waller conceded. 'But bribing Todd sounds feasible and, from what I've seen of him, Todd looks strong enough to knife an unsuspecting victim without any help from anyone. Any thoughts about the near fatality of Mrs Chambers? You said yourself Todd was a suspicious element in the accident. Having eliminated the whingeing girlfriend for Chambers, how about disposing of the wife?'

Hayes felt Waller was well out of depth with this conspiracy theory and tried to damp things down.

'But why would Todd shop Noel if he was in on it with him?'

'Poor sod thought his head was on the block and couldn't see why Chambers should get away without even being nailed as Prentice's lover.'

An urgent rap on the door cut Hayes' retort off short and he swivelled round as Waller's irritable 'Yes, what is it? I'm busy' rapped out.

Bellamy shot in, his hand held up in mute apology.

''Scuse me, sir. But it's just come in. Morry Chambers 'as wrapped his car round a tree just outside Pershore.'

'Dead?'

'Not quite. He's on the operating table. His sister's on the way to the hospital now.'

Thirty

'Hi, Pippa. It's Roger. Things are hotting up here and I wondered if you'd heard the news about Maurice Chambers being involved in a car crash. Delphi's gone up to be with him. Did she tell you?'

'Just half an hour ago. Poor kid's in a terrible state. She should never have driven off alone like that. What's her father doing I'd like to know? Even Johnny Todd could have given some support but even he's made himself scarce.'

'I can't talk now, it's all systems go here. I suppose Delphi taking off puts you on the spot with Brandt's recital tomorrow night.'

'And how! My boss is doing his nut – a fine bloody start to the festival and no mistake. Actually, it's not all bad, Brandt's agent's really on the ball. He's arranged for his regular accompanist to fly over from Hamburg today.'

'The Japanese girl?'

'That's the one. She's familiar with his repertoire and they can iron out the creases in the morning at the rehearsal rooms. Trouble is, it adds to the outgoings. We've got to pay for her flight, budget for an additional fee and, on top of that, set her up at the Randolph. But the agent's calling the shots, we've no alternative.'

'Look on the bright side, sweetie. Delphi running out on you could have scuppered the whole concert.'

'You are such a Sunny Jim, Roger,' she retorted with asperity. 'Ring me later, I'm up to my ears in it here.'

Bellamy came in and passed over reports on the extra legwork Waller had insisted on. Hayes glanced through the list and gave Bellamy a rueful grin.

'No interesting sightings then? No tramps seen lurking in the shrubbery?'

Bellamy shook his head, unsmiling, wishing he could get a handle on this new inspector. 'What shall we do about Todd?'

'Let him simmer, I've got things to do. Here, get Jenny Robbins to ring this number and ask for Sister Wooldridge. She knows me. I'm trying to trace the private investigator that Prentice used to trace Johnny Todd. Tell Robbins to ask if Mrs O'Brien remembers his name or the name of the agency. The old lady's got an eye for detail, she may know it. Angela Wooldridge will know how to question her without flustering the poor soul and I'd like to have a word with this PI – he dug up more than Todd's willing to admit. For all we know our suspect has a history he doesn't want us to delve into.'

Hayes rose to go, straightening his tie and reaching for his jacket. Outside the sun shone, the bright autumn light picking out the dust motes floating in the fusty atmosphere of the office.

'What shall I tell the Superintendent, sir?'

'Tell him I'm on my way to the village to speak to Noel Chambers. You'd better get your skates on, Bellamy, and do a thorough job on Todd's pad. Anything, anything at all, to link him with Prentice or the Chambers family. And see if you can dig up whatever it is Todd's anxious to keep to himself.'

'What sort of stuff, sir?' Bellamy replied with a degree of confusion.

'How should I know? Just use your loaf, man. Pick a decent team – Frazier's got a nose for a job like that. Take your time, there's no panic, Todd's not going anywhere.'

Hayes pushed past, anxious to get to the Old Rectory before Noel Chambers had grasped the significance of Johnny Todd being under suspicion.

The avenue of poplars was shedding its yellow leaves, the long drive up to the house carpeted with gold. Hayes felt buoyed up with the gut feeling that he was finally on to something.

A battered Rover was parked by the entrance, all the doors of the Chambers' garage block open to view. Only one vehicle was in place, a gleaming black BMW with a personalized numberplate which could only belong to Iris Chambers.

The door was opened by the housekeeper, who seemed visibly diminished by the sequence of tragedies befalling the family.

'Good-afternoon, Mrs Drake. Mr Chambers at home?'

'No, sir. He's gone to work. Terribly upset, poor man, but with Mrs Chambers out of action he had business to attend to . . .' Her voice petered out on a vague note, then she rallied, ushering him into the drawing room. 'But he'll be back soon – he can't leave Mrs Chambers alone for long. The vicar's with her now. That terrible accident with the piano all but crushing the poor lady was bad enough but now Maurice . . . Dear me, I'm dreading the next thing. Bad luck always comes in threes, doesn't it?'

Her mouth sagged, leaving her face puckered like a spent balloon. She left him alone and Hayes assumed his arrival would take a back seat until Noel returned. He glanced at his watch and decided to give Chambers fifteen minutes before chasing him up at his office.

He wandered over to the piano, where some sheet music lay open as if Delphi had rushed out in the middle of the piece. 'Fantaisie Impromptue' was an unashamedly pretty composition with an impressive number of notes, just the thing to bowl over the paying customers. He stared at the keyboard, lost in thought, and idly struck a few chords. The sound was surprisingly unbright, as warm as the golden October sunlight bathing the fading garden. His mobile phone jangled, shattering the mood.

'Yes?'

'Jenny Robbins here. I got on to Sister Wooldridge like you asked and she was terrifically helpful. Mrs O'Brien has taken to her bed, a throat infection she said but—'

'OK, Robbins, cut the cackle. Any joy on the private eye?'

Her voice came over in a rush, the words tumbling out like a split packet of peas. 'Absolutely. Sister Wooldridge said the old lady was anxious to help and gave her the key to her desk. Apparently Mrs O'Brien paid for the search herself and the final account plus the three reports on Todd were clipped together with correspondence from the solicitor.'

'So?'

'Mrs O'Brien said to post them to you but Sister Wooldridge suggested a fax would be quicker and I've got copies of all the reports here, sir. Shall I run them over to Newton Greys? It'll only take me ten minutes and there's stuff in there which will affect your interview with Mr Chambers.'

'Great work, Robbins. Yes, bring it over straight away – I'm still waiting to see him and I can't speak to his wife, she's closeted with the vicar.'

Jenny Robbins' driving was, as Hayes knew all too well, a bit too much in race-track mode for a panda car but the screech of tyres on the gravel was music to his ears. He hurried to open the door himself, mouthing placatory phrases to the housekeeper who appeared in the hallway, her pale features betraying an escalating anxiety.

'It's OK, Mrs Drake. Just another officer with some important papers. We'll wait in the drawing room, shall we? Mr Chambers won't be long now, I hope.'

Jenny Robbins looked flushed and crossed the hallway

with the eager footstep of a girl with the key to the castle. She glanced around the impressive room, taking in the chintz and fresh carnations, and bent down to retrieve the sheet music scattered in the fallout from her brisk entry.

They sat together on the sofa and were just starting to sift through the detective agency's file when the unlocking of the front door announced the return of the head of the house. They rose expectantly but Noel hurried through the hall and straight upstairs, presumably to report back to his wife, unaware of the police presence.

They subsided on to the sofa but before they could resume their examination of the report the vicar popped his head round the door.

'Ah, Chief Inspector. Mrs Drake told me you were waiting. May I have a word? The poor lady upstairs is very distraught. I said I'd hold the fort until Delphi phones through with some news. Noel is trying to cover several areas of crisis alone and your presence could not have come at a worse time, I'm afraid. Could you postpone your visit?'

'Absolutely not, Mr Harcourt. I'm not here in connection with Maurice's accident but a far more serious investigation. I must insist on speaking with Mr Chambers right away.'

'Are you sure?'

Hayes looked grim. 'Indeed I am.'

'Right then, shall I tell Mrs Drake you're happy to wait here for a few more minutes?'

He left them standing in the centre of the room and they exchanged glances of irritation before sitting down yet again to sift through Robbins' bag of tricks.

Thirty-one

Fifteen minutes later Noel Chambers joined them and suggested they move to his study.

The man looked drained; his tall figure, fleshed out with years of good living, seemed oddly off balance, as if life had finally struck a long-awaited blow.

He led them to a room at the back of the house overlooking an inner courtyard. No sunlight penetrated here and the dark panelling increased the air of claustrophobia. Hayes guessed this 'den' was not a regular bolt-hole for Chambers, a man who, despite his considerable affluence, appeared hardly in command of his beleaguered household.

'Please make yourself comfortable, Chief Inspector. I apologize for keeping you waiting, but naturally my wife is distraught. I'm afraid I have little to tell you about Maurice's accident, my daughter will telephone as soon as she has news. I presume there will be charges against the boy. Thank God no one else was involved in the crash this time.'

Hayes discreetly signalled Jenny Robbins to take notes and placed himself directly in front of Chambers, who had slumped at his desk.

'To put you straight, Mr Chambers, we are not here in connection with Maurice's accident. Our enquiries relate to the death of Sandra Prentice.'

The name barely caused a ripple of concern on the haggard features and his dull gaze answered Hayes with no more than polite interest.

Hayes leaned across the desk to place the agency report between them. 'You may not have heard, but we are questioning a suspect in connection with the crime. John Wesley Todd.'

This elicited a stronger response: Chambers took a pair of spectacles from his breast pocket and reached for the file. Hayes continued.

'As far as we have been able to determine, your son spent some time with Mrs Prentice on the afternoon of her death but claims to have been at home for most of the day. Perhaps you recall the afternoon in question: the fourth of October. Presumably Mrs Chambers discussed with you her quarrel with Maurice, which was occasioned by his admitted drinking bout with the victim at her house.'

'Yes, Inspector. An embarrassing family fracas, regrettably not the first. But Maurice has been spoiled all his life and Iris is alternately harsh and protective, which is destructive of any balanced relationship. But, yes, that day does ring a bell, now you mention it. Maurice was forced to stay in the study until I got home. My wife felt it necessary to distance herself from any possibility of an escalating row and, as has become all too apparent, Maurice in a temper is likely to drive off in one of our cars as this current accident only goes to prove.'

Hayes nodded. 'Let's get back to Johnny Todd. Tell me about your dealings with him.'

He looked bemused. 'My dealings with the piano tuner? Are you joking?'

Hayes tapped the file. 'If you would be good enough to study this report you will see what I mean. The investigation was made at the instigation of Sandy Prentice and I have reason to believe she shared this information with you.'

Chambers' mouth hardened as he skimmed through the PI's report, then pushed the file aside with a gesture of disgust.

'Shall we lay our cards on the table, sir? Johnny Todd was a close acquaintance of the dead woman and accuses you of being her lover. We suspect he was coerced into joining Prentice in her desperate attempt to nail you down. Do you deny your liaison with Mrs Prentice? A dangerous game, Mr Chambers, but hardly a criminal pursuit and I must admit that the case building up against Todd contains no evidence that you conspired in her murder.'

Hayes' victim fell back as if struck.

'You can't be serious! Me? Involved in murdering Sandy? I loved her. Yes, I know I'm a bloody fool to admit it but at least one thing Todd said is true. I loved that girl, and had recently broached the subject with my wife.'

'A divorce?'

'Perhaps. Eventually. Once we could agree on a settlement, but our business interests are complicated, not least by the role Maurice would continue to play after the break-up.'

'Mrs Chambers favours her son, I've heard, indulges him, as you mentioned.'

Chambers' hollow laughter struck a chilly note in that chilly room.

'Iris refused to take my proposal seriously, considering – as wives generally do so I'm told – that these "middle age crises" blow over given time. She was in no mood to agree to any divorce.'

'When Mrs Prentice found out about Johnny Todd,' Hayes tapped the file, 'she thought this would tip the balance in her favour. Discredit your wife in your eyes. Did you confront Mrs Chambers with her relationship with him?'

'Look, we're getting bogged down with this. You didn't know Sandy. She was a lovely, affectionate woman and everything Iris is not. I wanted to make a fresh start but when Sandy moved down here to live I knew time was running out. If I was to extract myself from my marriage without being taken to the cleaners, as they say, the procedure had to be carefully stage-managed.'

'You stalled?'

He nodded. 'I'm ashamed to say I dragged my heels a little, begged Sandy to give me more time. When she confronted me with this bombshell about Todd she thought it would turn me against Iris and give me something to bargain with. You see, my wife has built up a certain standing in the community and, believe it or not, has nurtured a genuine religious belief since we moved here. She's a churchwarden, you know, and having this unpleasantness exposed caused her real anguish. The vicar is with her now. Since poor Sandy died I have begged Iris to accept the situation and to bury it. We all make mistakes in life and acknowledging Todd would put it right. I even suggested we made him a full member of the family firm, for God's sake. I pointed out that I had been a real father to Maurice and opening our hearts to Johnny too would be no big deal. People are very forgiving.'

'You knew nothing of your wife's illegitimate son before Sandy found out about him?'

'Partly. Iris admitted she had another boy older than Maurice but he was a sickly child who died before she moved here to work as my secretary.'

The phone rang at his elbow. He grabbed it.

'Delphi! My darling girl. What's happened?'

They spoke at length, Hayes motioning to Robbins to sit tight.

Noel Chambers put down the receiver, all smiles. 'Good news. Maurice is going to be all right. A miracle of modern surgery. Delphi says he will eventually return to us almost as good as new.' He rose. 'I must tell Iris, she's been racked with torment over this.'

'I'll wait, sir. We haven't finished our discussion, have we? Johnny Todd is likely to be charged with murder –

my men are searching his house for the weapon as we speak. It's likely sufficient prosecution evidence will emerge within the next few hours and I was hoping that with the prospect of the support of your family he might decide to make a confession. The killing was a botched stabbing, in the pathologist's view, an accidental homicide which, with the right legal team behind him, would almost certainly be reduced to manslaughter.'

Chambers hesitated at the door. 'Yes, you're right. We owe that poor chap our support. I'll talk to Iris, get the vicar to back up your suggestion. But it may take a little time. Could you come back tonight, Chief Inspector?'

Hayes gave up, nodding to Jenny Robbins, who snatched up the agency report from the desk as they were hurriedly shown out.

They paused as Hayes unlocked his car.

'Did you believe all that?' asked Robbins.

'Noel only finding out about Todd being Iris's by-blow when Prentice stumbled on to it? On balance, I do. Sandy was counting on Iris being too ashamed to go public on her embarrassing first-born, not to mention her un-Christian ditching of a sick child while keeping her healthy boy. Iris Chambers has built up a valued status in the local community. I reckon Sandy threatening to tell the world would certainly be the trump card to persuade Iris to go quietly, to agree to the divorce and bribe Todd to fade out of the picture.'

'But Todd didn't agree to join Sandy in this game, did he?'

'Decent of him, if it's true. He's a stubborn bastard. But if he did refuse to co-operate Sandy could go it alone. Let's have another bash at Todd when we get back to the station. Here, give me that file, I'll ram it up his nose and see if he sings a different song from our Mr Nice Guy Chambers.'

Thirty-two

Bellamy was waiting for him. Hayes told Jenny Robbins to make herself available for the continuation of the Chambers interview that evening and she slipped off to decipher her notes. The two men repaired to Hayes' office and closed the door. He put on the lights, the dusk seeping in like a ghost at a wake.

'Well, how did the search go?'

'The good news or the bad, sir?'

'Don't bugger about, Bellamy, I'm not in the mood for your idea of repartee. Incidentally, where's Waller?'

'Went home to change for some civic cocktail party – something to do with the Oxford Music Festival.'

Hayes lightened up. 'Really? Can't see our superintendent with the cultural set myself.' He then outlined the state of play at the Old Rectory and pressed Bellamy about the search.

'Todd's house was an easy job, guv. Everything neat as a pin, no dirty washing up in the sink, not the usual bachelor pad in my experience and no evidence of any women on the scene. We didn't find any likely murder weapon but the tools in his van might fit the bill. Before we get round to charging him the forensic boys will have to pick over a whole bundle of implements. His desk was all in order an' all, accounts up to date, bank statements a bloody sight healthier than mine.'

'Any unusually big credits?'

'Difficult to tell. This piano lark seems to pay well and he's got a sideline hiring out instruments to concert halls. We could check with the bank manager to find out if he had a big cash business but with a service like piano tuning I reckon plenty of customers paid in cash. Frazier went through his VAT returns and thinks the bloke's a wizard with numbers.'

'Doesn't surprise me. For someone with just about the worst start in life, he's built up a decent living by sheer hard graft. Keeping the books straight fits my idea of a man with an ambition to get rich.'

Bellamy passed over a single sheet of notes attached to a blurred copy of a typewritten document. Hayes irritably shoved the lot aside.

'That's it? This is the only result of three senior officers putting a nit comb through a suspect's house, a place not only his home but his bloody office?'

Bellamy shifted nervously in his seat and jabbed a finger at the meagre paperwork. 'There was this, sir, a copy of Prentice's will. I tried to check with the solicitor but Mr Hardcastle felt it "inappropriate" to discuss it with me, though he did admit it was a copy of the authentic document. But we already knew about her will, didn't we, sir?'

Hayes pounced on the file and turned to the badly photocopied document, the print barely legible. He chortled, slapping his thigh with delight. 'And you found this in his desk? You're a bloody marvel, Bellamy.'

The sergeant looked thoroughly confused. 'You only said to look out for anything new connected with the Chambers or the dead woman, sir. This will's nothing to do with any of the Chambers or even Todd come to that – the person named is called O'Brien. I only put it in to bulk up the file seeing as we'd drawn a blank.'

Hayes jumped up, grinning like a lottery winner. 'You'll get a special commendation for this, Bellamy. Only goes to show what an experienced team can turn up from a load of dross. Get Todd up here in my office. I want to try a different approach.'

'In here? On your own, sir? He's a powerfully built bloke, looks like a gypsy to me. You'd be safer in the interview room.'

'Just get on with it, Bellamy, and tell Robbins to get up here with two mugs of coffee and to bring her report on the Chambers interview.'

Bellamy shook his head in disapproval but closed the door quietly; his understanding of Hayes' 'lateral thinking' – the stuff the new recruits rabbited on about after being on one of those new-fangled psychology courses – left him feeling out in the cold. Perhaps there were developments only Hayes' new flavour of the month, Robbins, knew about.

Five minutes later Johnny Todd entered the room, closely followed by a constable. Hayes invited him to sit down and waved the officer away.

'Everything all right, Johnny? No complaints?'

The ironic smile said it all. He sat opposite Hayes at his desk and crossed his arms, glancing round the sparse office with interest.

'Here's coffee. I gather you refused lunch.'

'How long's this going to take, Hayes? Am I being charged?'

'Not yet. We're just tying up a few loose ends. You're in deep shit, Johnny Todd, all of your own making, and as an intelligent man it must have occurred to you by now that it's time to come clean.'

'Is this being recorded?'

'No, it's not. I merely want to have an informal chat to clear the air. We got off on the wrong foot and before you start digging yourself deeper into the hole you're in I think you and I should start some straight talking. Let's go back to that afternoon when you called in to see Sandy the last time, shall we?'

Thirty-three

Todd sipped his coffee. Minutes ticked by before he started to speak, his voice low and with just the suggestion of a London accent.

'Here we go then. Like I said, I parked on the main road about three and she pulled me through to that greenhouse place at the back.'

'The conservatory?'

'Yeah. I was always telling her to keep the door through to the house closed because the damp from the misting equipment for the orchids wasn't doing her piano any good, but she took no notice, used the place as a general rendezvous.'

'She was already what you might call tipsy?'

'Over the limit certainly, and in a bad temper. She'd had to push out Morry Chambers just before I arrived, that loser would turn up like a bad penny all hours. I said I was busy and couldn't stay, which didn't improve things.'

'What did she want to talk about?'

'Same old stuff.'

'You tell me.'

'She wanted me to back her up.'

'To confront Noel Chambers?'

He squinted at Hayes in a calculating gaze.

'I wasn't Sandy's "heavy", Hayes, and I wanted nothing to do with it.'

'You refused?'

'You bet I did. Noel Chambers may look a soft touch but he's a powerful influence round here.'

'Quite. But Sandy had a fix on you, didn't she, Johnny? She suggested using the information she got from the detective agency to force Iris Chambers to agree to a nice quiet divorce.'

'I don't know what you're talking about.'

'Come off it, mate! Chambers admits that Sandy found out about your mother and she thought it was a way of getting you on her side over this.'

'You've lost me there, Hayes.'

'Well, just suppose I take it on trust that you wanted no part in putting the pinch on Noel by threatening to expose his wife's none too fragrant dirty laundry? I've seen copies of the agency reports, Todd. I know who your mother is.'

'So what? Iris ditched me as a kid and I've survived. Why would I want to diss her thirty years later?'

Hayes blew out his cheeks in disbelief. 'No grudges? Not so much as a temptation to pay the woman back? I'm not totally convinced that that so-called "accident" on the stairs with Delphi's piano puts you in the clear, especially when it turns out she told her first husband and also Noel that you'd died as a boy. Are you saying you didn't know she'd got you dead and buried as far as she was concerned?'

Todd flinched but refused to respond.

'OK, let me take my little scenario a step further. Sandy knew you as an obstinate sod, not easily pushed around, and when you refused to speak to Noel about your lousy upbringing she took a softer line. Said fair enough, no threats. Just go to Noel and tell him the sad story and suggest Iris might like to make amends, broadcast her reunion with her lost boy and give you a golden handshake to welcome you to the fold? Funnily enough, Noel now seems to think such an idea would appeal to his wife but Sandy knew her better, didn't she? Sandy knew Iris could never stomach the village gossip, the sly remarks of her smart county friends, that Iris would realize the only way out was to make a graceful exit, take the role of the poor abandoned wife whose husband's been seduced by a common hairdresser and agree to a settlement without any more ranting. She knew about the affair, you know; she just thought if she stood her ground Noel would go cold on the idea once he realized the costs involved. Betrayed wives of mature years walk away with a sizeable chunk of the assets, especially in Iris's case where it can be shown she contributed considerably over a number of years to the success of the firm.'

'I see what you're getting at, Hayes. You want me to admit to having an eye on sharing the Chambers fortune, don't you?'

'It's feasible, Johnny. Noel's willing to talk to Iris about bringing you into the family circle – not an unattractive offer for a lad brought up by the local authorities.'

Todd laughed, slopping his coffee. He placed the mug on the edge of Hayes' desk and wiped his fingers on his sleeve.

'You don't get it, do you, Hayes? When Sandy told me who my mum was and showed me copies of the agency reports, she thought she was doing me a big favour. That little bombshell just about broke my heart. Knowing myself to be blood-related to Delphi and Maurice was the very last thing I wanted to know. It took Delphi away more surely than death itself.'

'You wanted Delphi?'

'Of course I bloody did. I've been in love with that girl for years and now I find out she's my fucking sister.' Todd was almost in tears.

'You got mad with Sandy that afternoon?'

'I've already told you. We had a blazing row.'

'About Delphi?'

'Not just Delphi. Sandy had shared her so-called "good

news" with me months before that day and I learned to live with it. Fortunately, Delphi had never responded to my advances so no harm's done, but I wanted none of the Chambers lot, not their money nor their recognition, and I told Sandy over and over again to leave me right out of her little scam. If she really needed to wreck the whole Chambers family to get her man, I told her, he probably never intended to marry her anyway!'

'Whew! You don't mince your words, do you, Johnny? Why didn't you walk out on the whole situation? Leave Sandy to do her own dirty work and cut Delphi out of your life?'

'You think it's that easy? I've got a business, I need to make a living. By God, I've tried. Kidded myself she'd never find out about me being her brother, that Iris would let the divorce go through rather than let the whole bloody world know she had a history no better than the local teenage mothers she castigated in public at every turn. From what I've seen of my mother, I've come to the conclusion I was better off with Mrs O'Brien.'

Hayes doodled on the blotting pad, choosing his words with care.

'On that score, Johnny, what about this will business? You lied to me over that, didn't you?'

Todd frowned. 'The old lady's will? No, you misunderstood. I said I knew about the will; Sandy had told me, though she said Mrs O'Brien wanted it as a surprise bonus for me after she'd gone.'

'No, I meant Sandy's will. You said you knew nothing about Sandy making a will until I told you in the interview room.'

'Did I?'

'Don't play silly buggers, Todd, I've got it on tape. The fact is,' he said, passing over the sheets of legal documents, 'these were found in your desk this afternoon.'

'You searched my house? What right have you—'

'Shut up, Todd. This is serious. You knew all along that Sandy Prentice was leaving all her money to Mrs O'Brien. It doesn't take a mastermind to work out that if Sandy died first and after a decent interval the old lady passed away, you'd be the lucky beneficiary. How did you get hold of this copy?'

Todd visibly paled. 'Sandy showed it to me one day when I was tuning her Steinway – she kept all her private stuff in her filing cabinet and only got this out to show me what a big-hearted tart she was. She reckoned if I was halfway human I'd go down to see the old bird myself, give her a glimpse of me before she popped off.'

'You refused?'

'I've no time for slushy sentiment like that, but I was intrigued by Sandy's need to show off to me of all people. What did she have to prove? But I think she knew I saw through her, knew her to be a vulture underneath all that sweetness and light. Then she got called out to the conservatory to talk to the old chap from next door, to show him some new orchids in her collection. She was going on holiday the next day and wanted to put his hat on straight about the watering. I nipped into her back room where she keeps a clapped out photocopier for her bills and stuff and ran off a copy.'

'Why?'

Todd shrugged. 'Insurance, self-preservation if you like. Sandy had a hold over me and I wanted something to hit back with. I didn't believe she'd left everything to Mrs O'Brien – she'd only let me have a glance at one page of all the legal guff – and I thought there might be something in it I could throw back at her if ever she turned nasty.'

'But when you got home and had a chance to digest it you found out it was true. She literally had no one else to leave her money to at that time, did she, Johnny? It wouldn't take a smart chap like you more than a minute to suss out the next step though, would it? If Sandy got her way and married Noel the will would be scrapped.'

'So what? Even with her rackety lifestyle the chances of her outliving the old lady were more than a million to one in her favour, I'd say. What are you getting at?'

'You didn't like Sandy Prentice, did you?'

'She was a low-life scrubber pretending to be the village angel.'

'She had this information about you she wanted to use to lever Iris Chambers off the nest and, worst of all, she had thrown in your face the fact that Delphi's your sister. Did she taunt you with that? Had she guessed you were in love with the girl?'

Todd reared up, his face livid, and in a split second Hayes calculated that a fist fight in his office would certainly cause ructions with the constabulary and, at best, leave him with a broken nose. He pushed Todd back, eyeing him like a nervous lion tamer.

'Sit down, man! You're in enough trouble already. You had the opportunity and the motive to kill Prentice and you'll be charged first thing in the morning.'

'Murder?'

'If convicted it's a life sentence – no more music, no Delphi, no control over your life. Think on it, Johnny. You'll need a brief. A confession would be in your favour and mitigating circumstances will count for a lot.'

He banged on the door for the PC hovering outside and watched his suspect limp back towards the cells.

Thirty-four

Hayes sent Jenny Robbins home, warning her to be ready by eight that evening. 'I'll pick you up and we'll finish our conversation with Chambers.'

He drove back to Haddenham, grabbed a sandwich and showered before picking up the phone to ring Pippa. She wasn't answering and Hayes, remembering Waller's pre-festival drinks party, guessed Pippa was circulating with the wine and smiles. Poor girl. What a bore. All those civic dignitaries trying to pick something with which to entice their wives to give up an evening's telly from what even Hayes considered a pretty high-blown programme. He grinned, wondering if Florian Brandt had been frog-marched to Pippa's party.

His red-haired detective constable had changed too and wore a leather jerkin over a black polo neck and pale grey slacks. Together they presented a formidable team as Noel Chambers let them into the house.

'I sent Mrs Drake off for the evening; the poor woman's hardly had a moment to put her feet up since Iris came home from hospital. This won't take long, I hope, Chief Inspector?'

'Just a few loose ends.'

'In that case would your constable be kind enough to sit with my wife? She is in a very nervous state and has dismissed the nurse I engaged – can't stand hospitals and took an instant dislike to the agency nurse. The doctor is arranging something for me in the morning but if she could keep Iris company while we talk I could relax.'

Hayes exchanged glances with Jenny who shrugged, by no means happy to be pushed out of the picture. But Hayes decided that finishing off the Chambers interview and getting a signed statement would be merely a formality now that Johnny Todd was well and truly hooked.

'OK. If you feel it's important to keep an eye on the patient I can spare Robbins for half an hour.' He took Jenny's notes from her and waited in the hall while Noel led his unwilling stand-in nursie upstairs. Within five minutes they were once more closeted in the gloomy study.

Iris Chambers' bedroom gave Jenny pause for thought. She'd seen nothing like it outside the stately homes where, as a kid, she had been dragged by her starry-eyed mother, an enthusiast for brocade curtains and gilded furniture.

The woman propped up on pillows greeted her like a queen at a levee, inviting Jenny to pull up a chair and insisting on introducing herself simply as 'Iris'. Her face was chalk white and flecks of grey hair threaded the normally immaculate coiffure. Jenny wondered if this was the result of shock, Maurice's car crash being, according to Chambers, the knock-out blow to his wife, her own pain a secondary consideration.

'Tell me, Jenny dear. How is your investigation coming along?'

'I'm not sure I can discuss it, Mrs Chambers. Enquiries are still being made.'

'But Noel tells me that poor young man is likely to be charged with murder.' Her eyes continually flickered round the room and it occurred to Robbins that the woman's mind may have been temporarily unhinged since her near-death experience, closely followed by her favourite son's all but fatal accident. But maybe it was the drugs.

Jenny could not warm to this person who, to be fair, was

putting up a brave front, trying desperately to pull together a semblance of normality, even asking about her house-share with Pippa which Delphi had nearly joined.

'Noel is worried about Todd. It would be a miracle to discover him to be this alleged long-lost child after so many years, wouldn't it? Not that I believe it, of course. My elder son died. But I understand Todd is likely to allow this falsehood to become common knowledge. He's a strange young man, don't you agree?'

'I hardly know him, Mrs Chambers. He was more a friend of Pippa's.'

'We want to ensure he has the very best legal advice nevertheless. Pass me my address book, would you? It's in my briefcase on the chest of drawers. I would like you to give Todd the name of a really first-class lawyer I happen to know rather well. I can't believe that Todd is capable of murder. He hasn't confessed, I hope?'

'The case for the prosecution is being assessed. There was a motive, a financial motive apparently.'

'Nothing to do with that dreadful woman's blackmailing efforts to entrap my husband then? You found out about Noel's little romance I understand. A middle-aged fling as I see it. He met her through an escort agency, you know. Nothing but a common prostitute in my view.'

Jenny rose to fetch the address book, hoping to God Hayes would hurry up. This covert questioning by Iris Chambers was nerve-racking at the very least. How much was she allowed to discuss with a woman who seemed oblivious to the wickedness of her own part in Johnny Todd's life and obviously regarded him no differently since employing him as an up-market furniture remover?

With her back to the patient, Robbins rifled through a stack of papers in the briefcase, taking her time over it, scanning the numerous business contracts bearing Iris's bold signature. Then, with a slight recoil, her fingers touched cold steel. She withdrew a pair of barber's scissors, their small blades clotted with what appeared to be brown paint. She froze. Iris continued babbling away about Delphi's selfless abandonment of her important appearance at the festival the following evening.

'My daughter is extremely talented, as you know. And Noel has ensured she has had the very best tutors.'

Jenny replaced the scissors and went back to the bed, holding out the address book with trembling fingers.

'Would you excuse me for a moment, Mrs Chambers? I just want a word with my boss.'

She ran downstairs and rapped on the study door.

Noel opened it and instantly mirrored her anxiety with his own. 'Has something happened to Iris? Shall I call the doctor?'

Hayes rose from his seat, clutching a notebook.

'No, sir,' she stammered. 'Mrs Chambers is perfectly well. I'd just like a word with the inspector if I may?'

Hayes moved swiftly, sensing trouble, and closed the door behind him.

'What's up?'

'I've found the murder weapon. Sandy's scissors. They're in her briefcase. She must have taken them away from Maurice. We've only got her word for it that he came straight home after Sandy tipped him out before Todd arrived. He could have hung about watching the conservatory from the back field and gone back when the coast was clear. Iris could have cooked up the alibi about locking him in her study. She's a resourceful woman, sir, don't underestimate her now she's temporarily out of action. I reckon she's still in charge here.'

'But Maurice had no motive to kill Sandy. If Iris was protecting anyone, Noel was the one to want Sandy off his back.'

Jenny shrugged, even more confused, but went on to

describe her find, their whispered exchange in the dark passageway growing increasingly urgent. He sent her back upstairs, his mind racing, and returned to Noel's den.

'Would you mind if we postponed our little talk for the time being, Mr Chambers? My officer would like to confirm some facts with your wife. Did you realize Mrs Chambers is in denial over this claim of Todd's to be her son?'

'She's a sick woman, Chief Inspector, this medication would blur decision-making at the best of times; and since the additional trauma of Maurice's accident, accepting the unpalatable re-emergence of a son she had abandoned more than thirty years ago can never be instant, especially since Iris has long known him as a visitor to this house. There was never a moment's suspicion in her mind that Todd was who he now claims to be, and for all we know it may not even be true.'

'His name never caused her to wonder?'

'After all these years? And John's a common name, isn't it? It's not even as if the man bears the slightest resemblance to Iris, and he certainly looks nothing like Maurice. I have tried to discuss it with her but she refuses to budge. Insists the man's a charlatan. Nevertheless, from common decency Iris agrees we must do our best to secure him a good lawyer.'

'Robbins mentioned just now that your wife already has a legal contact in mind. Shall we join her? We can finish your statement later. I'd like to ask Mrs Chambers a couple of questions before she gets too tired.'

'Is this really necessary?' Noel glanced at his watch. 'I like her to get tucked up early. The poor woman needs all the rest she can get. Frankly, I'm amazed she has recovered so quickly, but then we often pulled her leg about her incredible energy. She's marvellously fit for a woman of her age.'

'Then we'll go up, shall we?'

Chambers reluctantly agreed and the two men followed Robbins to Iris's boudoir.

Thirty-five

Hayes pulled Jenny aside and quietly directed her to fetch an evidence bag from the glove compartment of the car. The two men went ahead, entering Iris's bedroom like a pair of bailiffs, their presence almost an affront in that over-furnished room.

Noel pulled up a chair for Hayes, who moved it in closer to where Iris's face was focused in the halo of her bedside lamp.

'I am so glad to see you, Chief Inspector. I wanted the opportunity to thank you. Noel tells me you probably saved my life. It would have been a farcical way to go, wouldn't it? Felled by a piano.'

She wore a lacy bed jacket tied at the neck with mauve ribbon and appeared assured, almost relaxed. Hayes guessed that being bedridden would be particularly frustrating for a woman of such vigour but, to all appearances, she was coping well.

'Mrs Chambers. May I trouble you to confirm the events of the afternoon of the fourth of October? I'm sure you remember it – Maurice said you arrived home early from the office and there was a row. He'd been drinking.'

Noel butted in. 'Is this really necessary, Hayes? Maurice has already been over it again and again.'

Iris raised a hand, putting on a brave smile, and said, 'Please, Noel. Let the man have his say. This will only take a few minutes, I'm sure.' She faced Hayes and began to answer, her voice low but in no way hesitant. 'You're quite right. Maurice and I quarrelled bitterly about his drinking and on that particular afternoon it ended with me leaving him to sober up, to sleep it off.'

'He never left the house?'

'Not that day, no. He was in no state to argue.'

'He says you locked him in your study.'

'Did he? Well, I suppose I did. Maurice is a temperamental soul and sometimes given to rather childish tantrums, especially when he's been drinking. It sounds draconian but I was fearful he might rush off in one of our cars if there was not a certain restraint, as his current situation only goes to prove. Maurice has written off Noel's car, you know. He was lucky to escape with his life but, thank God, no one else was involved this time. I imagine charges will be made when he leaves hospital.'

Jenny Robbins slipped in, discreetly placing an envelope in the DCI's hand before stationing herself on the other side of the room.

'Your son was seen crossing the field, presumably on his way home after depositing an empty bottle in the recycling bin in the village.'

Iris's eyes flickered with sudden interest. 'And this witness supports Maurice's statement? He or she saw no one else the police could haul in for interrogation? Well, that was decent of them. There are certain people in this village who hold a grudge against Maurice, people who would even perjure themselves to get him arrested.'

'Actually, being seen that afternoon doesn't constitute an alibi in connection with the murder. Mrs Prentice died before dusk, according to our expert.'

She brushed this quibble aside. 'Luckily I was at home that afternoon myself and you have my word that Maurice was incapable of leaving this house, as Noel will agree. Would you like me to make a formal statement? To confirm all this? I'm sure eliminating Maurice from this sordid inquiry will clear the air for everyone. You already have another suspect in custody, I hear. The man Todd. There is very little goes on in this village that isn't common knowledge in no time at all,' she added with a grimace.

'There is a new development.'

Hayes swiftly moved to the chest of drawers and searched the briefcase.

'What the hell are you doing?' she spluttered, her voice rising. He placed the scissors in the transparent bag, moved back to the bedside and held them out for her to see.

'These hairdressing scissors bear what appear to be bloodstains. Would you care to explain how they came to be in your possession, Mrs Chambers?'

'You're assuming they're Sandy Prentice's?'

'A reasonable conjecture, wouldn't you say?'

She smiled grimly but remained silent.

'These scissors were put in your briefcase with or without your knowledge?'

Noel wheeled round on Hayes, fear and anger bringing his normally bland features into dramatic focus. 'Watch it, Hayes! My wife's a sick woman. Making insinuations about Iris is just asking for a serious reprimand from your superior officers. This house has been in chaos ever since her accident, strangers coming and going all hours. Her briefcase was unlocked – anyone could have walked in here while we were visiting the hospital.'

Iris Chambers sipped a little water before turning back to face Hayes, her expression as serene as before. 'I think you've missed the point, Noel darling. The suggestion is that a member of this family hid these scissors among my private papers under the misapprehension that my bedroom was sacrosanct and that, with me unable to leave my bed, it would make an excellent hiding place. Quite where this fascinating exhibit was before would be a question I would ask if I were a chief inspector. But perhaps my reasoning is too awkward to fit into the slot our Mr Hayes has in mind.'

After a painful silence she turned her gaze on her husband once more.

'Noel, I want you to phone Father Peter. Ask him to join us if he would.'

'The vicar?' Jenny squawked.

Hayes shrugged, motioning Chambers to use the bedside extension so they could all hear. He was far from sure what Iris was up to. Playing for time maybe?

Well, it makes a change from calling for a lawyer, he reasoned. Finally, they were making progress.

Thirty-six

Noel waited in the hall for Harcourt to hurry over from the new vicarage built in the grounds when the Old Rectory was sold off. In a matter of minutes they had all assembled in Iris's room and Harcourt swiftly assumed a major role at the bedside. No greetings were made, no overtures from Iris broke the oppressive silence.

Jenny Robbins choked back an anxious query about formally cautioning Iris and waited for Hayes to make the first move.

'Perhaps I should explain a few details, Mr Harcourt. We are conducting a murder investigation and these scissors were found in Mrs Chambers' possession. She was about to tell us how they got there.'

All eyes focused on Iris Chambers. Her composure made her, in Hayes' view, not only a person of formidable mental and physical fortitude but capable of extraordinary self-delusion, her insistence that her disabled child had died only one example of her apparent amnesia.

Ignoring Hayes, she directed her remarks to Harcourt.

'Father Peter. You will be delighted to learn that Maurice's operation was successful. He is to make a full recovery. I spoke to his surgeon myself earlier this evening.'

'Wonderful news! Wonderful,' the vicar enthused, on the brink of launching into fulsome congratulations which mercifully Iris cut short, raising her hand in a cheerfully dismissive gesture.

'And so, in accordance with the promise I made, I shall have to place myself in the firing line, shan't I? The police seem to think a man called Todd is the guilty party but they've been thrown entirely off balance by the discovery of the murder weapon in my briefcase. Denying it would be time-wasting as their clever scientific tests will prove that the bloodstains on the blades are those of the dead woman. The trouble is,' she said, pausing, Robbins could swear, for dramatic effect, 'these unintelligent investigators are now thrown into confusion, and in their rush to bring someone – anyone! – to trial are likely to jump from the frying pan into the fire one might say, and accuse either my son or my husband of stabbing the wretched woman. Even one moment's logical thought would stop them in their tracks but I'm sure that would be asking too much, even though Maurice and Noel were clearly enchanted by our village witch.'

Noel leapt forward, grasping her arm. 'Here, hold on, old girl, you've said too much already and Harcourt's no bloody use to you, is he?'

She patted his hand and, smiling, pushed him away.

'On the contrary. Father Peter was my unknowing witness. I am a mother, a role closer to the human heart than even that of jealous wife. Until Maurice bolted and almost died in another of his appalling car crashes, I was unperturbed by the stumbling efforts of our local bobbies. They had tried to force my son to confess to the crime but had to admit defeat and release him. Quite right too. Maurice hasn't a violent bone in his body. But when his life hung in the balance I made a vow, a frantic mother's plea which must have been only one of many millions the Almighty receives every day. If Maurice lives, I prayed, I will lay myself at His mercy.'

'You told this to Mr Harcourt?'

'No, of course I didn't. I made a silent confession before communion which he gave this morning.'

'He came to the house?' Robbins sharply cut in.

She glanced scornfully at the girl. 'Naturally. Would you have me hobble to church on crutches, you silly creature?'

Hayes raised his hand in a calming gesture and urged Iris to continue.

'So there you have it. I killed Sandra Prentice and I do not regret it.'

Noel groaned and sank on to a Frenchified gilt chair, holding his head in his hands.

Hayes stood his ground. 'That's really not good enough, Mrs Chambers. Saying you killed this woman, possibly to protect your family, would not release Johnny Todd who is, after all, your son too.'

Harcourt had by now totally lost his cool and was fortunately rendered speechless.

Hayes held up the evidence bag like a holy relic and waited for Iris to respond. She seemed entirely in control of her emotions and eyed the quartet ranged at her bedside with studied calculation.

'Well, you might as well get it right. Unless I spell it out for you, Chief Inspector, there's no hope of you proving a case against me. And, frankly, for myself, now that life is reduced to essentials, the truth is the safety and health of my beloved Maurice is the only thing I care about.'

'And what about Johnny Todd? Would you have let an innocent man go to trial?'

'If I had not panicked and made this ridiculous deal with God, yes, Chief Inspector, I would. What you seem incapable of understanding is that my actions had nothing whatsoever to do with the wretched piano tuner and his greedy bid to claim a relationship.'

'Even in his present dire situation Todd has never expressed a wish to join your family or make any sort of claim on you.'

She tossed her head in cynical disbelief and tried to sit

straight, pain clearly etched on her drawn features. 'Noel, darling. Pass me those painkillers, will you? If I'm to get through this I shall need help.'

Noel reached for the bottle but she snatched it from him, impatiently struggling with the childproof cap before swallowing two tablets. Harcourt rearranged her pillows and at last the monologue continued.

'You were right about my terrible outburst against Maurice that afternoon. He came home reeking of alcohol and cheap scent and I knew immediately where he'd been. He eventually collapsed on a sofa and I locked him in, determined to have it out with that hussy once and for all. It was drizzling I remember but I was in no mood to be deterred by a few drops of rain and as the quickest way to that horrible new housing development is across the stubble field I grabbed Delphi's boots from the passage and rushed out. I could see the Prentice house from the footpath, all lit up like always, the illusion of party time for the stupid woman I suppose. The man she was with left, slamming the door behind him and stomping off through the side gate. I didn't recognize him and honestly didn't care. I was furious and I wanted to tell her in no uncertain terms that the game was up.'

She sipped from a glass of water Harcourt poured from a carafe on the bedside table. Noel looked up, waiting for the next bombshell, clearly shocked, but there was no stopping her now. In a strange way Iris Chambers seemed to have gathered strength from this confession, the gleam in her eye betraying a hint of triumph.

'I stormed in, skidding on the damp floor tiles in my muddy boots. She looked up, at first surprised, and then simply challenging in that bare-faced way of hers.'

'"What brings you here, Iris or can I guess?" she said, brushing her fingers through her hair. She thought she could get any man she set her sights on, you know, Noel. I still can't understand how a clever man like you could be so taken in. I got straight to the point, accusing her of ruining Maurice's resolve with her free booze and open house. She didn't deny it and once we got on to the subject of divorce there was no holding her. We exchanged insults across that ghastly bamboo coffee table and then, when she realized I was really not going to go along with the divorce, she calmed down and offered me a drink if you please! She said she had something to tell me.'

She sipped more water and reassuringly squeezed Harcourt's hand.

'Sandy Prentice was a whore but that wasn't the worst of it. She was a lying whore who knew I held all the aces. When it dawned on her that her threats to reveal the Todd scandal were not having the desired effect, she elaborated on my failure as a mother both to Maurice and this other so-called offspring. I lost my temper and said I would take her to court if ever she repeated those terrible lies.

'"Lies?" she screamed. "Lies? And who has lied to you for years? Not only your husband, who is beginning to bore me if you must know, but that sexy ex-con of yours, Maurice. Just lately I've found Maurice much more fun than his father, especially in bed. Maurice learned a lot of naughty tricks while he was in prison and they weren't the sort of games to impress his bloody mother," she said.

'I recall the bitch's words exactly. I reached out to slap her face, but she had grabbed her scissors from the table and lunged at me – I think she was even angrier than me. We struggled, I snatched the scissors and suddenly realized there was blood everywhere. She must have passed out. It was now getting dark and the two of us must have presented an astonishing sight to anyone using the footpath across the back field, but it seems nobody was.'

'You admit you accidentally slashed her neck? What about the wound to her thigh, the most serious injury and, according to the pathologist, the cut which severed an artery and bled profusely? You must have continued stabbing her as she lay on the ground.'

Iris shrugged. 'I can't remember that at all. I panicked. Before I knew what I was doing I had closed the blinds, turned out the lights and rushed away. It was only on the morning of my accident here that I discovered I still had the scissors – I must have dropped them into the pocket of my anorak in my haste to escape. I hid the beastly things in my briefcase, intending to dispose of them later, of course, but events overtook me and I lost the chance to get rid of them safely. Delphi's bloody piano tuner saw to that – I do believe he was trying to kill me.'

'To get back to the fight with Sandy,' Hayes insisted: 'what were your thoughts at the time?'

'No one had seen me arrive, and I guessed she would recover from what I assumed to be superficial cuts and decide, if she was sensible, that complaining to the police about two women brawling like fishwives would be an embarrassment to us both.'

She gripped the hem of the sheet, her voice dropping to a whisper.

'The days went by. I watched the lights in her house go on each evening and when no news leaked out that the damned creature had been attacked I began to feel safe, thinking she was lying low, possibly reconsidering her relationship with Noel and Maurice. Naturally, I had said nothing to anyone about our confrontation, convinced that "least said, soonest mended" would be the most sensible course.'

She looked Noel straight in the eye, her voice unwavering. 'I didn't know about the timeswitch on the lights or that no one had missed her. When the body was found I knew it was too late to make a clean breast of it, and trust that justice would prevail. Sandy Prentice deserved it, you know. She attacked me first with her damned scissors. Trying to take away my husband and ruin my lifestyle was one thing; debauching my son was unforgivable.'

'It wasn't true, Iris,' Noel croaked.

'Maurice assured us in his statement that he and Prentice were merely friends, Mrs Chambers,' Hayes said. 'If she taunted you with a lie like that it was pure frustration, knowing she had thrown everything she had at you in respect of your husband and the Todd business and it made no difference. But she knew your weakness, Mrs Chambers, and used it to hurt you in the only way that would strike home, through lying to you about seducing your son.'

Noel insisted on calling the doctor at that point and Harcourt ejected Hayes and his detective constable with no pretence of politeness.

Downstairs in the hallway, Noel hurried off to phone the doctor from his study and the Reverend Harcourt walked with them to the car.

'Did you believe all that, Mr Hayes?'

'The account of the murder? Yes, I did. What I found incomprehensible was this "deal with the Almighty". To confess to the killing in exchange for her son's life is like something from the Old Testament. You were as shocked as we were, of course.'

'Absolutely not. Such vows made in fear and panic are by no means unknown, especially in times of war. The fierce love of that woman for her son may seem exaggerated to the average person but her maternal protectiveness has been focused on Maurice for years. He's been a sore trial but his troubles only exacerbated Iris's need to save him from himself. A plea to God to give Maurice one more chance was an honourable wager. What was all that about Todd being related?'

'But she didn't confess to save Todd, did she?' Jenny Robbins insisted. 'Iris was prepared to let Johnny burn in hell if necessary and only confessed after I had found the murder weapon in her briefcase. Myself, I don't believe a word of this guff about any "honourable wager with God" as you call it. She's a resourceful woman and plans to play the "holy, holy" card to sway the opinion of the softies on any jury. And even if her so-called vow was, in a moment of despair, true, who's to say she was willing to honour it if the scissors had never come to light?'

Harcourt looked wounded, the determined cynicism of this young person clearly beyond his reach.

Hayes grinned, amused by the girl's feisty rebuttal of Iris Chambers' religious promises. She might even be right, but that would be for the prosecuting counsel to decide.

They parted under a starless sky, Hayes silently considering their next move. Todd must obviously be released pending a formal statement from Iris Chambers. Waller would be in two minds about this startling outcome and not a little displeased that the confession had been witnessed under such circumstances, leaving the legal experts plenty of room to manoeuvre.

He dropped Jenny at her gate. No lights glowed inside the cottage and for a moment the staunch policeman in him wished Pippa was at home. Iris Chambers' extraordinary religious logic was lost on him, sharing his incomprehension with his new love might shed some light on it.

'Let's hope the bloody woman doesn't take it all back in the cold light of day,' he mused.

Thirty-seven

Hayes drove straight on to Oxford, catching the Superintendent at the festival drinks party which, from the sound of it, was settling in for an extended celebration.

Waller looked flushed but expansive, exuding an undeniable irritation at being dragged away just when bonhomie was boozily overlaying what had started out as a tedious civic duty.

They found an empty office and Waller pushed him inside, snapping on the full panoply of harsh overhead lighting.

'What's all this in aid of, Hayes? Young Chambers croaked?'

Waller sat heavily on a desk, his bulk straining the maroon silk cummerbund covering the waistband of his evening trousers.

'No, sir. Maurice is out of danger apparently. That's the problem.'

'Eh?'

'I was at the house finalizing a statement from Chambers Senior when there was an unexpected development. A confession.'

Waller started up, clearly shocked. 'Noel Chambers admits killing the woman?'

'No! Not him. Here, let me explain.' Hayes moved forward, placing himself in the line of fire. Waller was not going to like this.

'Iris Chambers says she stabbed Prentice during the course of some sort of cat fight. Self defence. With Prentice's scissors.'

Waller glowered. 'Go on, spit it out, man.'

Hayes relayed the extraordinary turn of events, sparing Waller none of the bizarre details.

'You mean to say she admitted all this because of some cock-eyed religious nonsense? I've never heard such balderdash! Does this vicar bloke back her up?'

'He knew nothing about it.'

'Well, it's a new one on me. You don't believe it, do you, Hayes?'

'No, I don't, but she seems perfectly sane. It throws up a lot of problems, sir. The medics are going to say her mind was befuddled with post-operative drugs. And . . .' Hayes took a deep breath before serving up the final inedible morsel, 'I'm afraid events took on such momentum I hesitated to caution her.'

Waller closed his eyes in disbelief. 'You let her make this so-called confession without a caution? No witnesses?'

'Robbins was there, sir.'

'That young WPC? You left her there I presume? To keep an eye on the bloody woman.'

'Er, no. Mrs Chambers is bedridden at present, sir. Won't be running off anywhere.'

Waller stood, now coldly sober, fixing his new chief inspector with an unblinking gaze.

'Sometimes, Hayes, I wonder what I did to deserve an officer like you. Chambers could top herself, man! Send Robbins straight back to the house – make some excuse, we don't want to frighten the horses. First thing in the morning we'll take an official statement at the woman's bedside if necessary, but as soon as the doctors agree she'll have to be arrested, provided, of course, there are no more legal slip-ups. You did at least bag up the weapon, I hope?'

Hayes produced the evidence bag which Waller examined with the close attention of a man clutching at straws. He straightened.

'Right. I'll cancel my driver and the two of us'll finish this at the station. I want to go over every fucking detail tonight before we get it all screwed down first thing in the morning. Tell Robbins to inform the family we shall expect to interview Mrs Chambers at ten o'clock. That'll give her time to get herself a brief. Then we can start getting the real story. Do you think she's shielding that no-good son of hers?'

'Maurice? That's what we thought at first. Now I'm not so sure.' Hayes shrugged, his mind fizzing with the awful certainty that Iris Chambers was orchestrating an operation so devious that the police would eventually be forced to drop the whole thing, to let the murderer swim away from a whirlpool whipped up by just one clever woman.

Thirty-eight

The morning dawned sluggishly, rainclouds brooding overhead like a foretaste of the day of atonement. Waller and Hayes set out in the Superintendent's car on what would undoubtedly prove an impossible interview.

'If he's got any sense the lawyer's never going to let the woman open her mouth, and Chambers will be bringing in the medics to block any moves to charge her. It's a minefield, Hayes, and no mistake. How did that girl of yours swing it last night?'

'Robbins? Brilliantly. Slid back in without so much as a ripple. Discreetly confiscated all the medication after giving Iris her sleeping pill and sat by the bedside while Chambers knocked himself out downstairs with the whisky bottle.'

Noel Chambers let them in, his dishevelled state and bleary-eyed response that of an innocent bystander caught in crossfire.

'Good-morning, Mr Chambers. May I introduce Superintendent Waller?'

Chambers nodded and nervously dabbed his mouth, ushering them through to his study where they were introduced to a keen-eyed solicitor called Roberts. They grouped themselves around the desk, the lawyer taking a position behind Chambers, who slumped in his chair, saying nothing.

Waller took the initiative, outlining the police requirements in no uncertain terms. Hayes admitted a grudging admiration for the opening shots in what was likely to be a protracted war.

Roberts stood firm, backing up his defence of his client with a smooth refutation of the validity of 'a confession drawn from a sick lady suffering considerable stress as a result not only of her own state of health but the shock of her son's serious accident'.

'Nevertheless, I must insist on seeing Mrs Chambers myself, Mr Roberts,' Waller barked. 'My chief inspector here received a witnessed statement last night which cannot be ignored.'

The two men argued on, their demands escalating in legal jargon.

Noel had been silent throughout this exchange, his blood-shot eyes swimming in dazed incomprehension. Suddenly he spoke up, rising unsteadily to his feet. It struck Hayes that the poor devil had had the worst of it – a wife admitting murdering his mistress, a victim whom, by his own account, he had adored.

'Gentlemen,' he said thickly, 'why don't we stop this stupid bloody wrangling and see what Iris has to say?'

Hayes eyed the protagonists with interest, unprofessionally siding with the wretched husband. Reluctantly the lawyer agreed and the foursome moved upstairs.

Jenny Robbins stood uncertainly by the door as they trooped in, Iris, seated in a high-backed chair, looking suitably regal in a red silk dressing gown. She was surprisingly bright-eyed but was probably, Hayes concluded, the only one in the room who had had a decent night's sleep.

'My conscience is clear,' she said. 'I am at peace with God.'

Roberts frowned, hastily assuring her that she need say nothing.

Waller swiftly chipped in, stiffly introducing himself before launching into a series of formal instructions. He was just getting into his stride when the crash of the front door interrupted him. A sound of weeping seeped from the hall, galvanizing Chambers to make a lunge at the bedroom door and rush downstairs shouting:

'Delphi! Delphi, my darling, I'm here.'

Hayes hurried out, leaning over the banisters to catch a glimpse of the two figures slumped on a bench in the hall. After what he judged to be a decent interval he joined them, regarding Delphi's anguished features with alarm. But his daughter's distress seemed to have banished Noel's inertia and, cradling her in his arms, he looked directly at Hayes and muttered, 'There's been a development. We have to tell my wife.'

Resolutely, as if Delphi's return had given him back his true role on this tragic family stage, Noel supported the girl upstairs and, firmly pushing the lawyer and Waller aside, led her into Iris's room.

Delphi struggled to pull herself together and after a moment detached herself from her father's embrace. She sat on the edge of the bed and took her mother's hand. Iris had visibly paled, all bravado suddenly swept away. She whispered just one word:

'Maurice?'

Delphi nodded, the tears falling unchecked, her grasp of Iris's hand tightening.

'An embolism. Nobody's fault,' she croaked. 'A blood clot . . . the operation . . . There was no time to do anything. He didn't suffer, Mummy darling. It was all too quick. So sudden.' Her voice petered out.

The silence palpably weighted the atmosphere, and everyone focused on the broken woman in the high-backed chair. Iris continued to stare, unseeing, then slowly raised her eyes to take in the expectant faces. Her face darkened. She snatched her hand away, anger igniting like a firework in her head as she faced them all.

'You lied to me, didn't you, Noel? You lied. Pretended Maurice would live. And you too, Delphi. Liars, the lot of you. And I was stupidly taken in.'

Noel thrust himself forward, pulling Delphi aside and placing himself between the two women.

'For pity's sake, Iris. Why would we lie to you? Why pretend Maurice survived?'

'Because you knew he was all I cared about. You, Delphi, this house – everything! Why would I make that absurd confession if Maurice was dead?'

'You mean your so-called vow to the Almighty was just to cover for Maurice? Did Morry kill poor Sandy?' he screamed, starting forward and grabbing her arm. She furiously shook him off and for a moment the fire in her eyes wavered, but glancing round at the astonished listeners she drew her robe about her and, eyes narrowed, made a final thrust.

'Don't you dare accuse that poor boy!' she hissed. 'A killer? Maurice? Never. Not that I wouldn't have lied all the way to hell and back if he had. No, not Maurice. I killed that bitch Prentice and it happened just as I said. But a vow? A promise to God in exchange for my darling's life? What has God ever done for me? Tell me that! While Maurice lived – or I thought he would live – it was vital to protect myself with any means I could. All that religious guff would have helped me, touched the hearts of the simple-minded jurors who think they can tell the guilty from the innocent. A woman cheated on by a worthless husband? A grasping tart snatching not only the husband but seducing their son? Me, the faithful wife, defends herself from an attack from her husband's mistress only to find her son's life in the balance. Any excuse would have done but a pious prayer would definitely have saved me, persuaded the judge to be lenient, to bow to public opinion. Oh yes, my alleged deal with the Almighty would have claimed acres of newsprint, hours of televised debate and commentary, and I would have been pronounced "not guilty" or out of prison in just a few years. Years to share alone with my son, free from *you*, Noel, and your snivelling libido, free to make a decent divorce settlement and live comfortably ever after.'

She laughed, a harsh rattle in the throat, and Roberts moved in as if to break the spell. But she held him back with a dismissive wave of the hand.

'But Maurice is gone. I know it's true – a mother knows. I don't care to live any longer, even to live long enough to make fools of you all and escape on the coat tails of religious superstition. God played false with me, taking Maurice away like that, but I no longer care. Do as you please. I killed Sandy Prentice and I did it in hatred. No remorse. No prayers. Nothing.'

Thirty-nine

Hayes had to miss out on Florian Brandt's appearances at the festival and the Wigmore Hall, but eventually caught up with a performance in Amsterdam almost a year later. He booked a hotel room so he and Pippa could make a weekend of it.

After the concert they went for a stroll along the canals, comfortable in a love affair which had swiftly passed from fascination to passion without so much as a glitch over Hayes' unsocial working hours. She tried to persuade him to buy a piano from Johnny Todd and install it in his flat.

Hayes laughed. 'You think I'd stand by and watch that butter-fingered piano tuner push a lethal object like that up my stairs? Have a heart, darling. By the way, what's he doing these days?'

'Same old stuff. He's not the sort to let his mother's trial ruin his life. He was Iris's cuckoo in the nest. Incidentally, I've got some gossip about Delphi.'

'Yeah?'

'Seems she's lit out, enrolled at a conservatoire in New York. Good for her.'

'Broke away at last.'

'Well, I imagine her father's footing the bill, but the Old Rectory sold quickly so there's no shortage of cash.'

'Noel's moved to Aylesbury, I gather.'

'Alone?'

'Apparently.'

She laughed. 'That's the thing about living in a village: no secrets.'

'Well, Iris's secret stayed underground for years even though Todd was living practically on the doorstep.'

'He hasn't done any prison visiting then?'

'Todd? Visiting Iris? Not on your nelly. Anyway she'll be out in four or five years. She put on a wonderful act of contrition in the witness box.'

'Even without the "vow to God" malarkey.'

'No need. Noel was cast as the bad guy and poor Sandy Prentice got a rotten press so Iris got sympathy all round. And to be fair, she put in years of graft to make Chambers Autos a successful operation.'

'Will she break it up with a hefty divorce settlement do you think?'

Roger playfully rapped her knuckles. 'Nosy little thing, aren't you? Changing the subject, you remember that old chap who lives next door to the Prentice house, Mr Mason? Poor devils moved to the village expecting to find themselves in some sort of rural paradise. One thing struck me when I was talking to him. There were no birds singing in his new garden, he said.'

Pippa laughed. 'Weird, eh? Don't tell me you're getting superstitious in your old age, sweetheart. Incidentally, I heard on the grapevine that the Masons are moving back to the city. Can't stand all the blood and guts of country life, poor old things.'